LONG BOW

LONG BOW

Lauran Paine

CHIVERS

British Library Cataloguing in Publication Data available

This Large Print edition published by BBC Audiobooks Ltd, Bath, 2010.
Published by arrangement with Golden West Literary Agency.

U.K. Hardcover ISBN 978 1 408 45768 9
U.K. Softcover ISBN 978 1 408 45769 6

Printed and bound in Great Britain by
CPI Antony Rowe, Chippenham and Eastbourne

1

A SUSPICION

The ranch was huge even by standards of land-holdings west of the Missouri. Even in deeded land, mostly acquired from the railroad company who had been granted every other section of land as an inducement to lay tracks across the west, Long Bow was large.

It wasn't always patrolled by Long Bow riders. During the course of their riding they mostly only covered the parts of Long Bow where cattle grazed. Beyond those favoured places the land ran for many miles; northward twenty miles toward the mountains and for a fair distance up into them.

Westward, Long Bow crossed the north-south stage road to Cedarville and continued onward for at least ten miles.

To the west Long Bow's boundary went up, across and down the far side of what folks called the Arapaho Hills, which were a series of undulating upthrusts that tapered off over into Lost River Valley.

It was in the Lost River country where Long Bow had trouble. It was claimed by Indians and, being provident, opportunistic people whose livelihood from time immemorial had depended on game, and because Long Bow cattle were half wild, difficult to herd and leery of anything astride or afoot, the Arapahos made no distinction between private property and wild game when they killed Long Bow cattle.

It was a long-standing condition which Long Bow's founder, dead now these last twelve years, had resisted until it became clear that, short of having riders do nothing but camp in the hills watching, an expensive proposition, he rode to the Arapaho camp, sat down with the spokesmen and parleyed, not once but four times before the Indians agreed to take no more than ten cattle a year. Then Long Bow's founder, old James Welsh, rode home— a two day ride—cursing Indians and telling his rangeboss of those early days when the consarned Indians would kill as many Long Bow cattle as they felt like killing. The old man said, 'In'ians give promises an' sign treaties without any expectation of keepin' 'em.'

The solution was to keep Long Bow cattle away from the Arapaho Hills, something which could be accomplished without utilizing graze held apart for winter feed. It required an occasional sashay along the base of the Arapaho Hills, and in time this became a routine chore. Cattle were prevented from going near Indian country.

By the time the old man passed on and his unmarried son of the same name, James

Welsh, and pretty much of the same temperament and build, became owner and head of Long Bow, there were new winds blowing, and one of them was governmental policy of rounding up Indians, putting them on reservations and making them wards and dependants of the federal authorities.

The younger James Welsh had enjoyed a period of fewer depredations, at least as far as he knew, and had only once crossed the Arapaho Hills to confer with the Indians.

He had returned willing to accept solemn promises that in accordance with his late father's agreement with the Indians, they would take no more than ten beeves a year— and they had bitterly complained that only the occasional Long Bow stray came into their territory any more.

On the ride back Jeptha Cord, the Long Bow rangeboss, told Jim Welsh what old James had once said while making the same ride homeward.

'They'll slip to this side of them hills an' take what meat they want.'

Jim Welsh's reply to that was based on what he had heard in Cedarville. 'The army's rounding up In'ians all over the West. They'll get to this band in time. Jep, we'll keep cattle away from those hills an' Lost River Valley like we've been doin' since I was a kid. From now on In'ians are the government's worry.'

Jeptha Cord rode in silence for some

distance before speaking again. 'I don't know, Jim. In'ians know them mountains like I know the back of my hand. They'll know soldiers are comin' long before they get over yonder. Maybe the army'll catch some, but I'll bet new money they won't get them all. An' them as become holdouts still got to eat, don't they?'

Jim Welsh made no comment. Since childhood he had known the Arapaho. That they owned Lost River Valley even his father had never denied.

It was late spring with creek willows in full foliage, larks in the grass, magnificently clear days and cold nights. They had finally completed working the cattle, which required almost a full month. For a time saddlehorse work would be requisite, spring calving was progressing.

Long Bow employed five full-time riders and during the spring and summer they hired an additional four men, mostly what the riders disparagingly called 'overall men,' who did the haying, fence building, made winter wood; the myriad chores required but not the saddlebacking. That was done by the full-time men.

There was a ranch cook named Stub Morrow, an unshaven, overweight individual who chewed cigars but never lighted them. As ranch cook he was one of the best, but also like a talented person Stub was temperamental. Above everything else he would not hand anyone so much as a crust of bread between meals.

He lived in the bunkhouse with the riders—the 'overall men' had a separate bunkhouse and only the greenest of greenhorns would play poker with Stub, not entirely because he always won, which perhaps happened oftener than the law of averages allowed, but because when he lost whoever won from him was likely to be served undercooked meat, hard bread and watery coffee until he got over his annoyance.

Stub's position was secure. Jim Welsh's dry reply to a complaint one time summed things up well enough. 'Find me a feller who will replace him and cook as well as he does, and I'll think about making the change.'

Long Bow's yard was seven miles west and a tad north of Cedarville. Most of the time Long Bow riders and hired hands lived in isolation, which did not bother the older men but the younger ones fretted—not around Jim Welsh or the rangeboss but among themselves.

Long Bow ran 1,800 mammy cows with forty cows to a bull. With that many cattle a few could be missed at gathering time and often were, which occasionally resulted in riders finding a two-year-old unaltered calf riding cows. It required something like ten minutes to make the alteration which kept the calf hunched and unwilling to move much for a day or two.

But there were losses; any cow outfit as large as Long Bow and which ran as many cattle scattered over hundreds of miles of country, had losses. Natural losses to sickness and predators had been fixed by Jim's father at something like one half of one percent, a sustainable loss.

Long Bow cattle had, since Jim Welsh junior's ownership, imported good Durham bulls. Mostly the cows were every colour and design under the rainbow. Mostly too, they had impressive spreads of horns and the temperament inherited from generations of Texas and Mexican cattle, otherwise losses to predators would have been much higher.

They rarely feared a man on foot and were not above challenging a mounted man, but a gunshot over their heads or in the dirt which flung little stinging stones and earth into their faces resolved challenges without exception, and the Durham bulls, raised under close supervision from birth, did not cause trouble. In fact it became the custom to start a bull or two in the right direction, which they would willingly follow, in order to get the other cattle to follow.

With that many cattle, riders became able to tell some cows from the others. It was partly their markings but it was also their characteristics. Some threatened by dropping their heads and pawing, others were overly protective of calves—those were the dangerous ones—and some were herd-bolters, animals who would trudge along obediently enough until they came to a dense thicket, then charge full force, eyes closed, and whose momentum would carry them so deeply into the thickets it was very difficult to get them out.

An old rider named Barney Miller once said that cows were like people; a big crowd of them are just animals, but every one as an individual possessed a different personality and character, and he was right. All a person had to do to make this discovery was handle a sick cow, snake-bit or with a maggoty broken horn, or with a knocked-down hip from fighting, in a corral where the critter was alone. The really odd thing was that often the handler of those quarantined animals discovered that they had the same personalities as some person they knew or had known.

Barney Miller was a top hand. He was straw boss upon the rare occasions when Jep Cord was not around. Bunkhouse sages had been guessing Barney's age for a long time. When some rude individual would ask pointblank, Barney would smile, point to the distant mountains and say, 'They was a hole in the ground the day I was born.'

Barney and a younger man named Tad Butler were a roping team. In time anyone could learn to rope on foot, but good teamropers were rare. For Barney, team-roping was a blessing, a man did not have to jump off his horse and throw some 500- or 600-pound calf by himself. One team-roper headed, the other heeled. It was done from the saddle. Barney and Tad Butler were the best. They could put a 1,400-pound animal on the ground stretched full length in about the same time a roper on foot could catch a calf.

Barney had been with Long Bow seven years. He knew the range, the cattle, the seasons and the routines as well as anyone, including his boss.

He chewed tobacco, was quiet, keenly observant and at times melancholy. He had once owned a small ranch, with a good woman and a young son to help. Everyone makes mistakes. Barney Miller's mistake was to build his house, barn and corral in a broad, tree-shaded canyon. In '76, the same year which was bad for a man named George Armstrong Custer, an unprecedented flash flood had put Barney's canyon under eight feet of water. He found and buried his son but never found his wife.

The crisp morning Jim Welsh called Barney and Jep Cord to the main house was one of Barney's bad days. It had been such a spring day years earlier when the flash flood had destroyed his hopes and his happiness.

The reason Jim had summoned his rangeboss and Barney had to do with

8

something he had heard the previous day on a trip to Cedarville. He explained it curtly. 'Sam Ewart at the general store told me Will Devon over in the cottonwood creek country told him he'd been raided of about fifty head. He said Will trailed 'em most of one day an' got shot at by what Will told Sam seemed like a whole damned army.'

Jim got them coffee which Barney sipped in silence. Jep said, 'How long ago?'

'Three days,' Welsh replied. 'Sam said Will rounded up some men around town an' went after 'em again.'

Barney leaned to put his cup aside as he said, 'An' they didn't find 'em.'

Jim nodded.

Barney nodded. 'They drove 'em east?'

Again Jim nodded.

Jep gazed at the older man. 'Railroad, Barney?'

'That'd be my guess,' Barney said and smiled ruefully. 'Things change, don't they? When I was young there wasn't no railroad to load stolen critters on so's they could be out of the country in a day or two.'

They finished their coffee and sat quietly for a time before Jim said, 'I'll go see Will, but it seems to me that might be a one-time raid. Anyway, we're seven miles from town an' Will Devon's place is another twelve miles or so east of Cedarville. They most likely won't come back. They'll raid somewhere else, but all the same . . .' He smiled at the other men who nodded in understanding.

Outside on their way to the corrals Jep said, 'That's pretty slick, ain't it? Who'd think to have cattle cars parked on a siding with an engine waitin'?'

'It's somethin' old-time rustlers would give an arm an' a leg to do, but there wasn't no steam cars in those days. Jep, the world is changin' an' so far I can't say as I like it.'

They left the yard in a group to scatter later and ride through bunches of cattle. It was a mite early for screw worms but there were always late-calving cows, which rarely posed problems, but first-calf heifers could be counted on occasionally to go down from straining with a first-born calf, and unless help arrived both heifer and calf would die.

It was something Long Bow riders did on a consistent scale. With so many cattle there was always something. If it wasn't a hung-up heifer it was an old mammy cow with a wobbly baby whose after-birth had attracted coyotes or, worse, wolves.

The men rode armed on those far-flung sorties, but ordinarily around the yard or at the working corrals and branding ground no one needed the awkward weight or interference of a sidearm.

This time when the riders scattered Barney rode due north and Jep sashayed easterly. It turned out to be a long day, the last rider to return to the yard was Tad Butler who arrived late, off-saddled with one hand, cared for his animal the same way then went to the bunkhouse where shadows were forming and someone was firing up the lamp when he walked in.

He had blood on the front of his shirt where his right arm was cradled. The arm was bloody too.

The others got whiskey. Barney gently drew out the bloody arm, told a rider to hold the lamp close, looked long then leaned back to ask Tad Butler two questions. 'How long ago, an' where did it happen?'

Tad was pale, sweating and disoriented. 'Happened when I got off to pee over near In'ian Rocks. The horse was faunchin' about somethin' but I didn't see the damned rattler until it hit me.'

'How long ago?' Barney asked.

'Two, three hours ago . . . I slit it crossways and squeezed blood out.'

They put Tad into his bunk, covered him, tried to feed him but he wouldn't eat. Someone went after the bottle on the bunkhouse table but Barney said, 'No! He's had enough.'

The rider protested. 'Whiskey's what folks is supposed to drink as soon as they can after bein' bit.'

Barney glared, turned his back on the rider and put a worried look on his team-roper.

11

'You kill the snake?' he asked, and Tad dully nodded, closed his eyes and breathed hard.

Later, after Jep went to the main house to tell Jim Welsh what had happened, Jim said, 'Ride to Cedarville an' fetch back the doctor.'

'It's nighttime, Jim.'

'I know that.'

'I've seen 'em snake-bit before. If they make it through a day an' a night they'll live.'

Jim did not argue, he said, 'Bring back the doctor, Jep!'

After the rangeboss had departed Jim went down to the bunkhouse. A 'breed Indian rider named Four Feathers stopped him at the door with a finger across his lips. 'He's sleepin'.'

Jim went to stand beside the bunk looking down. He told them he'd sent Jep for the doctor. The 'breed rolled his eyes. If rattlesnake venom got into a man's blood he died. Maybe not immediately but eventually. Sometimes when they lived through they had problems as long as they lived.

Barney stirred fire in the stove, placed the speckle-ware pot over the burner, got a cud tucked into his cheek and sat at the table where he could see his roping partner. He was still sitting like that when Jim Welsh left, by which time the coffee was hot. They filled cups and stood like owls. Someone filled a cup for Barney and put it on the table. Barney did not touch the coffee.

A rider named Pert Scovall, a Texan, raised

an eyebrow in the direction of Four Feathers. The 'breed barely shook his head, which was his way of saying leave Barney alone.

Jep returned with the medical man a little short of first light. He'd had to hunt him down; he'd been south of town delivering a baby.

The doctor was grey, rumpled, lined and weathered. He did not ride horses, he drove them. He was a widower, a Secesh veteran of the war, never very neat, sometimes cranky, but vastly experienced.

He examined Tad thoroughly, draped his coat from a wall peg, pulled up a stool, sat down and looked at the solemn riders as he said, 'Is that coffee still hot?'

They brought him a cup. Barney spoke from the table. 'Will he make it?'

The doctor looked hard at Barney. He knew who he was from seeing him often in town, but that's all he knew. He answered like someone who'd been asked that question a hundred times.

'I think so, yes. He cross-cut the fang marks and squeezed blood out. If he did that quick enough he likely squeezed out some of the venom. What's his name?'

'Tad Butler,' Barney replied. 'Anythin' you can do to better his chances?'

'Just set, wait and watch . . . That's gawd-awful coffee!'

2

PUZZLES

Tad made it but was sickly and weak as a kitten for about two weeks. Barney fussed over him like a mother hen. Four Feathers told Pert Scovall that Barney should have been a squaw.

When Jim returned from the long ride to the Devon outfit, he visited the bunkhouse after supper, dropped his hat atop the table and said, 'Barney guessed about right, an' accordin' to Will Devon there was maybe six or seven of them. We talked. He's put his three riders to goin' armed, hired an In'ian to watch for tracks, an' said the next time he'll chase 'em to the gates of hell. Two of the critters they rustled were pure-bred redback cows he'd bought only two months ago.'

Jep had a question. 'Can't he go to the railroad people an' find out who they was an' where they took his cattle?'

Jim nodded. 'He's leavin' tomorrow to do that. He said it don't make sense unless the railroaders were workin' with them, an' the more I thought about that on the ride back, the likelier it seemed.'

Jim picked up his hat, he was dog tired. The last thing he said before leaving the bunkhouse was, 'Until he gets back we won't know any more'n we know now . . . but we're at least a long day's ride from his place.'

Someone else was interested, a rawboned large man named Winfield Evans, the town marshal of Cedarville. He arrived at Long Bow the day following Jim Welsh's return from the Devon place.

He was a clear-eyed, gangling man with a reputation from backing down from no one. He had a drooping moustache, a slit of a mouth and rarely wore his badge. He didn't have to, after nine years as local lawman everyone knew him. He was a slow-talker. When he and Jim Welsh had a watered whiskey on the long porch of the main house, he said, 'Dangest thing I ever heard of. Rustlers, sure; we've always had 'em. But usin' the steam cars . . . seems to me these lads is experienced at their work. Will Devon's In'ian tracked 'em six miles north-east where there was a corral an' a loading chute at a siding. Jim, it don't seem to me men would go to all the trouble of haulin' down poles an' buildin' a chute an' a corral just to make one raid.'

Long Bow's head man hadn't heard the details of the raid. This was the first he'd heard exactly how the rustlers had taken the cattle away. The longer they sat with coffee in the morning warmth, the more he was inclined to accept the lawman's opinion. What clinched it was when Win Evans also said, 'There's somethin' else—you know Arthur Knowlton

15

down at Clarendon?'

Clarendon was a good-sized town on the railroad line twenty miles south of Cedarville. Jim knew Knowlton because he operated the bank down there, the only bank for 300 miles in any direction. Jim's father had helped found that bank, had used its services to the day he died, and Jim also used it. He said, 'Yeah, I know Art Knowlton, knew him when he come along a few years back an' took over. What about him?'

'Well, seems he cashed a pretty big voucher for a feller . . . I forget his name . . . from Denver anyway. A livestock buyer.'

Jim frowned as he turned toward the lanky man. Before Jim could speak the marshal raised an arm. 'Who's that?'

Jim looked. 'Stub Morrow the cook.'

'Yeah . . . I expect I should've known. I've seen him come to town with a wagon.'

Jim got the discussion back where he wanted it. 'About this feller who cashed the voucher—how big was it?'

'What I was told by Sam at the store, it was for one thousand dollars. Seems like an awful lot of money to me; don't it look that way to you?'

Jim's patience was wearing thin. 'It is a lot of money. What else did Sam hear?'

'That this feller told the liveryman down there he was a cattle buyer.'

Jim waited. When the lanky, slow-talking

16

man just sat there watching Stub arrange laundry over a lass rope stretched between two trees, Jim finally said, 'Anything more?'

'A little. Last night I met Will Devon in town an' asked him how much them fifty head would sell for. He said close to six hundred dollars. Ain't that a tad high?'

It was a tad high for fifty head but as Jim refilled their coffee cups he wondered if whoever the cattle buyer was, had other expenses. He asked if the lawman remembered the cattle buyer's name and got a drawled response. 'I do now, for a fact. It was Burt Moody . . . You ever hear of him?'

Jim shook his head as he tasted the coffee.

Win Evans said, 'Neither have I, an' I been here long enough to know just about every cattle buyer who comes through.'

Jim put the cup aside and testily considered the other man. 'Win, Devon's cattle was shipped away, out of the country most likely. You can't tie some feller down at Clarendon to them.'

'Sure you could, Jim. Rustlers got to be paid for cattle. Hasn't been no cattle shipped out down yonder at the siding since last autumn. This Moody feller wanted the money to pay for cattle; Will's critters is the only ones been shipped out since last autumn. You see?'

'No exactly.'

The lanky man slowly turned to regard Welsh. 'If it's a gang of rustlers . . . maybe like

17

them gangs of high-binders like they got back East. They operate like it's a business—hire the rustlers, get the cattle shipped out, an' pay off fellers who done the stealin' . . . you see?'

Jim settled back gazing down where Stub had appeared with another bucketload of wet wash.

He would need time to ponder all that Marshal Evans had said; right at the moment it sounded far-fetched. As the lawman jack-knifed up to his feet he looked down and smiled. 'What I rode out for was to say maybe you'd best look a little out. Remember, they still got that corral an' loadin' chute over yonder.'

Jim went down to the tie rack with the lawman. When Win was astride and evening up his reins he said, 'You got an awful lot of land with cattle scattered from hell to breakfast . . . I'd have riders poke around if I was you. Thanks for the coffee.'

Jim went to the bunkhouse where Tad Butler was recuperating by playing solitaire and drinking Irish coffee. Tad looked well enough but when he went to the stove for the coffee pot Jim noticed that he didn't track very well.

They visited but not for long, Jim had something on his mind besides bunkhouse conversation. On his way to the main house Stub appeared carrying his bucket full of spuds from the root cellar. He put the bucket down and said, 'Old long'n lean come out to say we're missin' cattle?'

Jim shook his head. 'Just visitin', Stub.'

As Welsh continued toward the house the cook looked after him, shook his head, picked up the spud bucket and went over to the cookhouse. A feller couldn't work for someone as long as Stub Morrow had worked for Long Bow and not get to know the head Indian pretty well; something was bothering Jim Welsh.

When the riders came in there was a setting sun behind them. Jim waited until they had been fed then called Jep and Barney to the main house, told them about the marshal's visit, told them what Evans had said and while it seemed a little chancy to him, it might not be a bad idea to make forays among the herd from now on when there was time, and maybe drive the animals a few miles closer to the home place.

On the way to the lighted bunkhouse after their visit with the boss, Jep said, 'They'd have to build a corral an' a chute. There'd be no other way to get cattle into the railroad cars, an' that means they'll be back. My guess is that they'll know they stirred up a hornets' nest raidin' Devon. Unless they're dumb as dirt they'll go raid a long way from hereabouts before they come back.'

Barney did not comment until they were on the bunkhouse porch, then all he said was,

19

'Jep, I'm havin' a hard time figurin' how they done that. A railroad cattle car?'

Jep laughed. 'Things're different, Barney, for a fact.'

As Barney was reaching to open the bunkhouse door he said, 'But that don't make 'em any better, does it?'

The following day Jim rode to Cedarville to hear from the storekeeper if what the marshal said was true. Sam Ewart was a man who once had been able to shoulder-lift a yearling but age and a sedentary occupation had turned muscle to fat. He had a nice fringe of reddish hair around his head low down and not a sliver of hair on top.

He was a genial man, prosperous and well thought of. He'd come to Colorado seventeen years earlier to establish a stage company franchise, bought the store instead and had never regretted it. Sam was a widower with a grown son back East in school.

He took Jim Welsh to a dark little office at the rear of the store, sat him down, offered a cigar which Jim declined, eased down into a squeaky swivel chair and told Jim almost exactly what the marshal had told him—except for the part about the corral and the loading chute.

Jim had a question. 'How did you know about the transaction at the bank?'

'Young feller who clerks down there came through a couple of days after Knowlton an' the cattle buyer did their business. Young feller named Weston. He handled the money transfer. He told me the cattle buyer had never been in the bank before. I was wonderin' if Will Devon ought to know.'

Jim didn't think so. 'He's gone to talk to the railroad people. Maybe what he'll come back with will make you tellin' him unnecessary.'

Sam Ewart smoked his stogie, slowly inclined his head and spoke through a fragrant cloud of bluish smoke. 'I didn't know he'd gone to that. Jim, I'll tell you somethin' Win Evans an' I figured out last night at the saloon them steam cars run on rails, they can't just up an' go off on their own, an' there are way stations every few miles. It come to Win to maybe ride up along them rails an' find out where a cattle train passed along an' with luck where it stopped to unload. How's that sound to you?'

'Sounds fine, Sam, unless that train went all the way up into Wyoming, in which case Win's clothes might be out of style by the time he got back.'

Jim picked up the mail, bought as many things he thought Stub might need which could be carried on a saddlehorse, and left town in mid-afternoon.

When he reached the yard several of the riders had come in. One of them was Barney Miller. When Jim was caring for his horse he heard someone behind the barn at the corrals telling someone else to make the damned horse stand still.

He went out back and stopped in his tracks. Barney was getting Tad to mount a horse. Tad was swearing and his jaw muscles rippled. Jim watched as Barney held the horse still for Tad to mount. Tad had a little trouble but with a boost in the seat from Barney he made it. His entire bearing changed. Jim laughed and walked out there. Barney turned defensively, 'He's well enough.'

Jim had no trouble with that. He looked at the mounted man. 'How do you feel?'

Tad's reply was not quite as firm as he intended it to be when he answered. 'Ready to ride in the mornin'.'

Jim took Barney aside to say, 'Not tomorrow. Not for another few days.'

Barney nodded agreement and as Jim left the corral Barney told his roping partner to make a few sashays around the corral. When Tad did this Barney leaned on the stringers watching. When Tad came up Barney said, 'That's enough for now. Get down,' and watched as the recuperating man dismounted, a little clumsily. Barney said, 'I'll take care of the horse. Go on over to the cookshack.'

Tad hesitated at the gate, looking at the older man. 'Tomorrow, Barney?'

The straw boss was pulling the latigo loose with his back to the gate when he replied, 'Not tomorrow, another three, four days. Go on over to the cookshack.'

When Barney finished with the horse he tucked a sliver of Mule Shoe into his cheek and leaned in the barn doorway for a while. There were lights in the cookshack and muted noise. Barney spat amber, hitched at his britches and instead of going to the cookshack, went to the bunkhouse, rummaged his possible bag until he found a faded tin-type of a woman standing with a half-grown boy. His son would be about Tad's age by now, if he'd lived.

Barney did not go over to the cookshack, he took the half-full bottle of whiskey out back to sit in the evening's pale light and sip now and then.

By the time the riders returned he had put the bottle back in its place and had walked out a ways to await the arrival of the moon.

Only Pert Scovall wondered aloud what had happened to the straw boss. The 'breed answered. 'He goes out by himself when the moon is good.'

That ended the comments about Barney's absence and when he returned they had a game of pedro going, waited until he was seated and dealt him in without any comments.

For seven days routine work filled the time of the riders. Jim rode out with them twice. Only one untoward event occurred. Barney and Tad came upon a pair of wolves feinting an old one-horned cow who had a frightened and bewildered calf at her side.

The old girl's tongue was hanging out, the hair around her eyes was sweat dark. She had been holding the wolves off for some time before Barney and Tad crested a low timbered hill and saw her.

Barney dismounted, tied his horse, went to the farthest tier of trees, raised his six-gun chest high and with his left hand pressed firmly against a tree he aimed.

Behind him, Tad did the same but he was a little slower. They both missed the first shot, the noise of which put the wolves into a belly-down run. Tad shifted position, aimed a tad high and fired. One running wolf went up into the air, came down in a grey ball and rolled until he fetched up against a rock, dead as he could be.

The other wolf got beyond handgun range. The old cow was pumping air like a bellows. When two riders came out of the hilltop timber after the gun-fire, she swung around to fight them too. Her little wobbly calf clung close. It did not see the mounted men.

Barney stopped, leaned on the saddlehorn and smiled. 'Next time, old girl, calve closer to the yard.'

They turned back leaving the cow safe with her baby. She watched them out of sight. Tad said, 'Danged habit they got of goin' off to calve. If she'd been with the herd them wolves wouldn't have stood a chance.'

Barney got rid of his cud, spat and boosted his horse over into a lope. Tad followed the older man's example. When they had rooftops in sight Barney said, 'I know that old cow. Three years back she had twins. Quite a sight seein' a calf on each side suckin' for all their worth. It don't happen often.'

When they reached the yard the sun was gone, there were noises from the bunkhouse and lights in the cookshack. They were caring for the animals when Stub stepped out to the porch and, using a discarded shoeing hammer from the smithy, struck someone's handiwork which consisted of a bell-shaped creation with two horseshoes welded around the bottom. When struck the contraption made a bell-sound loud enough to be heard a mile from the yard.

When Barney and Tad walked in there were nods but no greetings. Stub placed a large coffee pot in the middle of the table, looked at Barney and said, 'Where you been?'

Barney was seating himself when he looked up in surprise. 'Where I always been—ridin'. What's the matter with you?'

Stub didn't answer, he was fully occupied at the table, but Jep Cord spoke after flushing food down with black java. 'Will Devon come by. He told Jim the railroad folks said they didn't know anythin' about an engine haulin' cattle cars. When Will told them what had happened an' how it was done, all them railroaders said was, it couldn't have been no train of theirs, and showed him a book of schedules. They didn't know a damned thing about no stolen cattle nor no train haulin' cattle away. All they could tell Will was that if such a set of cars used their tracks the time Will's cattle was hauled away, it had to go north because a scheduled train was comin' from the south.'

Barney ate in silence. He and Tad were the last to leave. As they were rising Stub came from his kitchen wiping both hands on a soiled towel. Stub said, 'Maybe that train flew away.'

It was such a ridiculous remark neither Barney nor Tad replied to it. Stub followed them out to the porch to say something else. 'If them folks back East can set two steel rails in the dirt an' run steam cars from back there to out here on 'em give 'em enough time an' they'll figure a way to make them steam cars fly—then where would we be when the rustlers come?'

At the bunkhouse the customary after-supper game of poker was in progress. It was a hurried game. Usually Stub required better than an hour to set his cookhouse to rights after supper, which meant he would not be able to join the poker session for a while and no one was unhappy about that.

The following morning Jim rode out with the others. He and Jep split off easterly. Barney and Tad went north-easterly. The others hung lower and rode due east. The idea was to find, and bring closer to the home place, any cattle they saw. The idea had been Jim's. He did not say whether he had been motivated by Win Evans's visit or his talk at the store with Sam Ewart.

But it required no great amount of sagacity to understand why any easterly critters would be driven miles westerly. If raiders figured to rustle Long Bow stock, it was Jim Welsh's intention to make it as difficult as possible. He was not convinced they would come, nor was he convinced they would go as far as they would have to ride to raid him; there were other outfits, some of them on the east side of Cedarville coach road where rustlers wouldn't have to drive cattle so far.

Jim's problem was that although he could make it difficult for raiders coming from Will Devon's direction, Long Bow had hundreds of bunches of cattle grazing in other directions and actually, the critters north-easterly grazing along the foothills were not very far from the roadway.

He told Jep they would take a wagon, go northward in a few days and drive those Long Bow cattle westerly too.

Jep didn't object but deep down he felt all this caution was taking time away from regular chores. As far as he was concerned those rustlers wouldn't raid in the same area twice—unless they were fools—which they were not, but while driving cattle westerly with the day ending, Jep still thought the precaution was a waste of time.

He remained convinced no one would build a corral and a loading chute then abandon them after one raid, but all this pushing cattle westerly so soon after the Devon raid seemed both premature and not entirely necessary to him.

Cattle thieves would scout up a country, and Long Bow would be a lot farther to drive rustled beef than it had been to drive them from the Devon outfit. There were other things that needed doing.

He was both right and wrong. For a fact there was other work that needed doing.

3

SKUNKED

Four Feathers arrived in the yard late on a Friday evening. The others were over at the cookshack and missed seeing him ride in.

He did not even pause at the bunkhouse, he went directly to the main house where Jim, who was doing paperwork, responded to the knocking on the door, and led the 'breed to the parlour. He offered him a drink which Four Feathers declined—he hadn't eaten since sunup. Then he spoke plainly to his boss. 'Them In'ians from Lost River was scoutin' up cattle from back in the timber couple miles east of Arapaho Hills.'

Jim gestured toward a chair. Four Feathers ignored that to also say, 'They seen me settin' on a knoll watchin 'em. When I headed back they was still in the trees, mostly out of sight but they was still there.'

Jim was not very surprised. The broncos had to eat, they had pretty well exhausted game in Lost River Valley years back. He asked how many were in the northerly timber country.

Four Feathers answered frankly. 'I didn't count 'em but I'd guess maybe eight or ten. They're after cattle sure as hell, an' that many could carve up quite a few cows and haul the meat away.'

Jim asked the 'breed to send Jep to the main house and thanked him before seeing him to the door. Four Feathers went directly to the cookshack where the men stopped eating to look up; the 'breed's face was set in a bleak expression. He told Jep Jim wanted him and sat down, shoved back his hat and piled a plate, lowered his head without a word and ate like a starving man.

When the rangeboss reached the main house and had been told what Four Feathers had seen, he thought a moment before saying, 'If Feathers saw 'em this afternoon an' got

29

back here after dark—what can we do?'

Jim considered that while awaiting Jep's appearance. 'Go up there in the morning. If they butchered critters we can trail them by the dripping.'

Jep nodded. 'Then what?'

Jim sat down and motioned for the rangeboss to do the same. As Jep sat, hat in both hands between his knees, Jim said, 'It depends on how many cattle they butchered. One or two isn't enough to go over there fired up to fight. I wish the damned army would get around to takin' care of things like this.'

Jep stayed with the point of their discussion. He had no faith in the army's arrival; maybe someday, but Long Bow's problem was right now. He said, 'Jim, one or two this time, four or five next time, an' later, eight or ten head.'

Welsh nodded, unconvinced but not happy. 'In the morning, guns all around; we'll go up there after we eat.'

'They won't be there.'

'Then we'll track 'em until we find 'em.'

Something made the rangeboss uncomfortable. 'If we ride into their camp loaded for bear, they'll know why an' there's a hell of a lot of stronghearts over there. I figure the odds would be about like the ones Custer had.'

Jim was briefly silent, then said, 'We'll go north anyway. If we leave about dawn we should get to the hills by maybe one o'clock . . .

How about Tad?'

As the rangeboss was rising he said, 'He ain't real strong yet but pretty near.'

'If you got doubts, Jep, leave him behind.'

At the door Jep grinned. 'Maybe you could tell him he can't go but if I told him he'd saddle up anyway.'

When the rangeboss got back to the bunkhouse all the riders were there, solemn as owls. Four Feathers had told them. Jep draped his hat from a wall peg, got some coffee then told them what Jim had said. He did not look at Tad while speaking, not even when he told them they'd carry along their saddleguns as well as their beltguns, but if he expected Tad not to notice that he was not being spoken to, he was wrong. As soon as Jep had said everything Tad went to the space between his bunk and the next one, took down his booted Winchester and leaned it at the foot of his bunk.

Barney and the rangeboss exchanged a look. Jep shrugged and that settled it.

Stub was not included; nor was he indignant, not about that anyway, but he was irked when Jim came to the cookshack later and told him to have breakfast ready an hour early. Stub nodded but as soon as Jim left the cookshack Stub swore like a trooper.

It was dark and cold when the riders stamped into the cookshack where Stub, splayed unlighted cigar clenched, brought food

31

to the table in a foul mood. No one teased him; none of the riders were in a teasing mood.

When they went to the barn to rig out Stub went to the porch to watch the puny lantern light they used to get ready by. Four Feathers was in the best light. Stub chomped his unlighted stogie wondering what it must be like to be half-tomahawk rigging out to maybe ride to a fight with full-bloods.

After the riders left the yard, hunched inside coats, heads pulled low like turtles, Stub went back to the warmth of his cookshack, rolled up a sleeve and groped elbow-deep in a flour barrel. He gripped the bottle by the neck, drew it out, took a half cup of black java to the table, and tipped in the whiskey. Removing the stogie and raising his feet to a bench he relaxed, totally and fully. There were advantages to being a cook; he wouldn't have to hide the bottle again until maybe evening. It would take the riders and the boss that long to reach their objective and return.

The cold was only slightly less this late springtime dark morning than Colorado's winter mornings, but as Barney had once said, cold was cold, whether it was below zero or twenty degrees above.

A couple of the riders rolled and lighted smokes. Jim did not use tobacco. He had tried it once behind the barn when he had been thirteen, and had been so sick he thought he'd die and wished he would. For the hundredth time he watched Barney, who was riding stirrup with him, tuck a cud of molasses-cured into his cheek and shuddered. He had once tried that too, and the result had been even worse. He had thrown up right down to his boot straps.

Two hours later with false-dawn increasing visibility a little, Jim loped out. The others followed. It was barely possible to make out the first foothills with their ranks of stiff-standing pine and fir trees. From here on Four Feathers took the lead. He did it at a steady walk without looking at the ground until visibility had improved, then he suddenly stopped and raised an arm for the others to also stop.

As clear as a bell there was a gunshot from some distance ahead. After a brief lull there were two more gunshots. Four Feathers leaned on his saddlehorn peering ahead when Jim came up and halted beside him. After several minutes without more gunshots Jim said, 'That didn't sound like In'ians shooting cattle.'

Four Feathers agreed by nodding but said nothing, sat as still as a statue looking ahead.

There was a sudden fierce exchange of gunshots. Four Feathers said, 'Saddleguns,' and this time it was Jim who agreed without speaking.

Barney came up scowling. 'What in the hell is going on up there? That's too many guns for eight or ten In'ians.'

No one answered. Another sharp exchange occurred, this time with those firing seemingly moving easterly. Only one more shot was fired. It seemed to come from the direction where the first exchange had occurred.

Four Feathers handed Jim his reins, got down, lifted the Winchester from its boot and walked away. Jim dismounted, the others followed his example. There was no talk as the men stood bunched and tense.

Eventually Barney spoke. 'That wasn't In'ians shootin' at each other.'

No one commented until Jep squatted beside his horse straining to see ahead and softly said, 'Listen! Off to the east. Can you hear it?'

Barney irritably said, 'Hear what?'

'Cattle. Listen.' Jep came upright looking eastward across the seat of his cantle. After a long moment of silence he exploded. 'Son of a bitch! Someone's drivin' cattle!'

Barney still heard nothing. He said, 'In'ians? Which way?'

Jep snarled at the older man as he was toeing into the stirrup. 'In'ians your butt! Lost River Valley is west. You're deef as a post, Barney. Can't you hear them cattle bein' driven east?'

Pert Scovall couldn't hear anything either but he kept his mouth shut and got back astride. Four Feathers appeared in a hurry. He scarcely even grunted when he slammed the Winchester into its boot and sprang across leather without even testing the cinch, which was loose. He raised a rigid arm. 'Rustlers! They're a hell of a distance easterly.' Four Feathers took the lead again. No one questioned that, least of all Jim Welsh. Four Feathers wasn't a top hand but in a situation like this he was more likely to be knowledgeable than any of the others.

Barney rode back with Tad Butler, almost as concerned with the condition of his roping partner as he was with what was happening in the dusky dawnlight, which was beginning to get a steely look to it, which increased visibility, but not nearly as much as the men following the 'breed would have liked.

Four Feathers eventually slackened pace, and when Jim came up the 'breed said, 'No good,' and repeated it in Lakota. 'Dina sica.' He raised his arm again. 'Too far, I can't see no dust.'

Jim made no comment but as poor as the light was no one could have seen dust.

What all that gunfire back yonder had been about was not lost in this fresh development. Jep rode grimly silent. He had been wrong about cattle thieves returning so soon after the Devon raid but at the moment that was not even a pinprick to his conscience. Later it would be but no one would remind him, which was just as well.

When the sun arrived as abruptly as a seed being popped out of a grape there was visible dust but it was so distant it appeared as ground-mist which it couldn't have been this late in the season.

They were riding tired animals. Four Feathers' exasperation drove him to cursing in two languages, then intermixing them, which would have caused laughter any other time.

Jim slackened to a kidney-jolting trot, something no horseman on this side of the ocean ever used for very long. Jim eventually slackened to a walk as he spoke to the others. 'We're too far behind. They must have been moving cattle before that fight started back in the trees.' No one dissented. In fact no one spoke at all. Every one of them was too exasperated to speak. Jim added a little more. 'Directly we hit the north-south stage road, better go south to town an' get fresh animals.'

Barney was disgusted. 'Hell, we'll lose 'em if we do that.'

Welsh turned on the older man. 'They're already too far ahead. We keep pushing these animals we're goin' to end up on foot.'

When they reached the road Jim turned southward. His riders followed, as silent as stones.

By the time they had Cedarville's rooftops in sight the sun was clear of the easterly curve of the world. By the time they got fresh animals from a bewildered liveryman, answering only a minimal number of that aroused man's questions and were heading north-east again, the liveryman went over to the café which had its usual crowd of breakfasting townsmen and told them what he had gleaned, which was simply that raiders had made off with Long Bow beef.

Within a half-hour the news had spread, and while everyone was indignant, few proposed getting saddleback to join the rustler-hunt.

It would not have made much difference; by the time the Long Bow riders were on the trail, clearly marked by sunlight, any townsmen who had got astride would be so far back they would not be able to find the Long Bow riders. Someone headed for the Devon ranch to spread the news, but even that couldn't provide much help. By then the sun was well up and climbing. However, Will Devon got his riders a-horseback, picked up the well-marked trail and followed it, but not in haste.

The Long Bow men were loping along the base of a timbered hill when a rattler lying in their path gave its warning sound and Four Feathers, out front, did not hear the snake but his horse did. First it shied violently and Four Feathers, caught unprepared, barely had time to grab the apple before the horse bogged his head and bucked. Four Feathers let out a bawl and sailed through the air like a crippled bird, landed on his all-fours, half stunned, and the horse ran for all it was worth with Barney shaking out a loop as he chased it. He made the catch, yanked the horse hard with two dallies, then turned and led it back.

Barney was mad. As he stopped beside the 'breed who reached for the reins, Barney said, 'Damn In'ian,' re-coiled his rope and rode back where the others were waiting. He turned in beside Tad and growled, 'They do better on a pad saddle an' a squaw bridle.' He raised his voice. 'Let's go.'

Four Feathers rode with Pert Scovall, Jim took the lead. They hadn't needed a sign-reader since sunrise. The trail was wide and trampled. As Jim rode he tried to estimate how many Long Bow cattle the rustlers were making off with. He settled on fifty-sixty head, told himself he could be off fifteen head either way and loped steadily until Pert Scovall, standing in his stirrups, yelled and pointed ahead.

The inevitable had happened. It wasn't possible to push cattle as hard as horses. There were three head-hung cows up ahead, indifferent to everything except their own exhaustion. They turned, tongues out slobbering, too tuckered to be afraid.

Barney called to Jim, 'That brockle-faced cow—Tad an' I know her. We run off wolves baitin' the old girl.'

The men stopped, sat their saddles soberly considering the nearly wind-broke trio of cows. Barney said, 'She had a calf.'

Scovall replied dryly, 'Ain't no baby calf could keep up,' which was the gospel truth.

Jim dismounted, turned easterly with his hat tipped low and said, 'Too far. We're never goin' to catch 'em . . . son of a bitch!'

Not a word was said. It wasn't just the disappointment, it was also their boss's acceptance of what they had come to bitterly believe right after sunrise—when there were plenty of tracks but no sighting and no dust.

They were about as far from Cedarville as the distance between the town and the Long Bow yard, about seven miles. When they turned back Jim explained to Devon what had happened. Devon rode a short distance before his perplexity made him ask a question. 'Who was they fightin' back yonder?'

Four Feathers answered. 'In'ians, but when you think back, it must've been whoever they had watchin' their back trail. It wasn't more'n two or three. The others was pushin' the cattle.'

That thoughtful deduction held them all quiet except Will Devon. The Long Bow men were impressed by the 'breed's reasoning. Devon said, 'Same way they did at my place. I'll tell you, gents, they aren't greenhorns.'

Barney was disgusted all the way through. 'Then why'n hell are we ridin' to town? We can't catch 'em, but sure-Lord we can find their loadin' chute an' tear it down.'

'They'll be gone,' Pert said, and Barney exploded. 'Course they'll be gone but we can fix it so's they won't be able to raid our country again for a long time . . . Jim?'

Welsh was slow replying. 'We'll go to town, get our own horses back and eat at the café. We're skunked so wastin' a little more time isn't goin' to hurt. Besides, I'm hungry enough to fight a bear over a dead fish.'

Will Devon left them when his buildings were in sight. Another mile or so they encountered four town-riders armed to the gills. Jim told them the same thing so they also turned back.

Marshal Evans was at the café when the glum Long Bow men walked in. He nodded, continued eating until they were all seated then said, 'I got one of 'em at the jailhouse.'

At the abrupt silent stares this announcement caused, Win Evans sipped coffee and put the cup down before saying more. 'He ain't in real good shape. The 'rapahos brought him in, said he was worth thirty dollars because him or one of his friends shot an In'ian. I gave 'em thirty dollars . . .' He looked at Jim. 'You want to see him?'

Every Long Bow rider arose to follow the lanky town marshal. As they passed through the door the caféman said, 'What'm I supposed to do with your food?'

Barney turned to answer. 'Keep it warm. Someday we'll be back for it.'

40

Barney was in the middle of the road with the others so he didn't hear the caféman's sulphurous remarks.

Win Evans unlocked his jailhouse and led the way inside. Most *juzgados* had a separate room for the cells. Cedarville had not modernized its jail since it had been built years back by hide-hunters and trappers. It was one large room made of logs with a low ceiling, one window, a gunrack and one fairly large strap-steel cage.

When the Long Bow men entered Marshal Evans went to stop in front of the cage and jutted his jaw in the direction of a pale-faced, rumpled, unshaven, unwashed man lying on a wall-bunk who did not move when his visitors lined up looking in.

Someone had set a broken arm and bandaged a wound inside a torn trouser-leg high up.

Evans unlocked the door, stood aside as the Long Bow men went past, and took his place at the foot of the bunk as he addressed the wounded man, 'These here are the gents you'n your friends stole cattle from.' He then said something that was absolutely untrue. 'They came to town to hang you.'

The man on the bunk moved sluggishly, rolled his eyes at the Long Bow men and spoke in a slurred voice. 'You better hurry.'

Win Evans looked down his nose shaking his head. 'You ain't goin' to die, mister. The

41

midwife who patched you up said you lost a mite of blood but them injuries ain't even bad enough to keep you from singin' Yankee doodle.'

Jim stood beside the bed and asked the man his name. The answer he got surprised no one. 'Name's Abe Lincoln. What's yours?'

'Jim Welsh. I own the ranch you stole those cattle from.'

Abe Lincoln's sunk-set expressionless eyes fixed on Jim. 'The army'll get them damned In'ians of yours, and maybe you for harbourin' 'em.'

Jim found a three-legged stool and sat. 'What started the fight up yonder?'

Abe Lincoln answered with some vigour. 'Them damned In'ians you had sneakin' around in the timber. Some of 'em come down an' tried to cut out eight or ten of our critters. It was too dark to know what was goin' on until one of them broncos let out a yell. Then the fight started. But the cattle was already a mile or such a matter easterly. The fellers watchin' the back trail fought back, then run for it . . . How'd you know to have them In'ians up there waitin'?'

Four Feathers spoke from an impassive face. 'In'ians can smell rustlers five miles off. You're lucky they didn't catch you . . . In'ians take hair of rustlers.'

Barney and Jep were looking at the 'breed, his expression had changed as he spoke. It

42

became coldly menacing. Under other circumstances Jep would have laughed. When it was required of him Four Feathers could do an excellent imitation of a bloody-hand warrior. He had been raised by missionaries. He grew up more white than Indian, but since whites expected Indians to be fierce, stoic people, Four Feathers had over the years perfected the look and even, upon occasion, the pidgin-English whites associated with Indians who knew their language.

4

PUTTING PIECES TOGETHER

Abe Lincoln or whatever his name was had no outstanding characteristics except sullen defiance. He had a raffish, unwashed, unshorn appearance. In size he was average in all ways.

He was tough. Had to be to live as he lived. That he had never lived within the law was obvious. The longer he talked the more he gave the impression of an individual who scorned the principles other people lived by.

When the lanky lawman asked if he had dodgers out on him, he said, 'That's for you to find out,' and made a tired smile which the others interpreted correctly: Abe Lincoln had many names and changed them as frequently as other men changed shirts. Tired, gaunt and worn down though he was, he instinctively defied everyone who did not live as he did—by the gun, by rustling on dark nights, by just about everything dishonest and deceitful.

Jim Welsh asked about the other rustlers and Abe Lincoln replied predictably. 'I don't have no idea what you're talkin' about—In'ian lover.'

Marshal Evans sauntered to the bedside, leaned with a smile and hit the splintered arm. The prisoner exploded in pain and anger. He rolled up on to his side to protect the arm. Evans caught him by the shoulder and flung him back over. He still smiled as he raised a knotty fist. The pain had to be excruciating when he again struck the broken arm. This time he leaned with both hands to prevent Abe Lincoln from rolling away. He said, 'Straight answers, you son of a bitch, or I'll bust the other arm.'

They glared at each other but the outlaw was not only in pain, he was also feeling poorly. For ten seconds they remained like that before the marshal spoke again. 'How many of you damned cow thieves are there?'

This time the answer came quickly. 'Seven.'

'An' who's your head In'ian?'

This time the outlaw hung fire. 'What head In'ian, you scrawny bastard?'

The knotty fist came down hard. Abe Lincoln cried out. He feebly struggled to roll sideways but Evans held him pinned by the shoulders. He was still smiling. 'Once more—who is the head In'ian of you thievin' bastards?'

'Burt Moody. You hit me again an' I'll catch you out someday.'

The threat hadn't sounded very convincing. Marshal Evans released the outlaw, straightened up still smiling. 'It's goin' to take more luck'n you'll ever have to keep you from gettin' lynched. Who is Burt Moody?'

Abe Lincoln was grey, in pain and frightened. 'He's a cattle buyer.'

'Is that a fact? From down south, is he?'

'From Wyoming.'

'How did you fellers get a train to haul away them stolen cattle?'

This time Abe Lincoln showed something very close to demoralization when he answered. 'All we done was find the cattle'n drive 'em to where they could be loaded. I don't know nothin' beyond that.' Lincoln rolled his face toward Jim Welsh. 'You ain't got no right to beat prisoners. They got fee-lawyers in Denver—'

This time Marshal Evans did not use his fist. When his open hand struck the outlaw's face it sounded like a small pistol shot. Evans was no longer smiling. 'In this country,' he said, 'folks got no use for rustlers. All I got to do is leave the door unlocked an' go for a horseback ride. They'll haul you out of here an' hang you from the baulk over the front openin' of the livery barn. It's been done before.'

'You're a lawman,' the outlaw protested. 'You got to protect your prisoners.'

'That's a fact,' replied Evans. 'An' I do protect 'em . . . all but horse thieves an' cattle rustlers. How long you fellers been doin' this . . . usin' steam cars an' all?'

The outlaw was sweating. He also seemed to be getting confused and disoriented, from the additional pain. 'All I tell you is that me'n some friends was hired by Mister Moody to scout up cattle.'

'Who built the corral an' loadin' chute?'

'We did. Train hauled in logs'n Mister Moody showed us what he wanted.'

Jim Welsh listened. He had a question. 'This Burt Moody—what do you know about him? Where he came from an' all.'

'All I know is that he's big, hefty feller with black eyes, black hair an' beard, an' wears britches and coats that match, smokes stogies an' don't almost never smile. He's all business. I'm pretty sure he's from Wyoming.'

'Pays you well, does he?'

'Pays better'n range wages by a damned sight.'

'Where are you from?'

'A place called Royalty in Nevada.' The prisoner paused. 'My paw worked in a mine over there. My maw died of the consumption. I was sixteen. My paw left the mines. I never saw

46

him again.'

The Long Bow men watched the bitterness seep into the prisoner's expression as he said these things. But it was something else he said that startled them. 'Mister Moody's got other fellers doin' the same thing we been doin' up in northern Wyoming an' over in Idaho. He's a damned smart man.'

Jim Welsh said, 'Sounds like it. Where does he peddle the cattle?'

The outlaw had no idea. 'Like I told you, us fellers scouted up cattle, drove them to the siding, loaded 'em an' Mister Moody paid us cash on the spot. I got no idea where the cattle went.'

'What do you know about the railroad?' Welsh asked, and got a blank stare.

'But you meet Mister Moody some place?'

'Yeah. He gives us the name of a town an' we go there. He shows up, an' we go to work again.' For the first time the outlaw showed something close to satisfaction in his expression. 'He's a real smart feller. It goes off slick as grease.' He paused to look at Jim Welsh. 'Except this time. How'd you know to have the tomahawks in the trees when we come along?'

Jim rose, jerked his head and led the way out front where Win Evans made a clucking sound. 'He didn't really tell us much that we didn't know, did he?'

Barney spoke. 'Yeah he did.'

47

'Some names is about all,' Evans replied.

Barney looked straight at the lanky man when he said, 'This here Moody feller, sure as Gawd made green apples, is the same feller who cashed them vouchers down at Clarendon.'

Evans nodded. 'That don't take much figurin', Barney.'

'For a fact it don't,' the older man agreed. 'But somethin' bothered me from the first.' Barney faced Jim Welsh. 'If you was a stranger an' walked into a bank with a voucher for a thousand dollars, you reckon they'd cash it without knowin' a lot more about you than you wear pants an' a coat that matches an' got a beard?'

Jim was slow replying. 'Art Knowlton; is that what you're getting at?'

Barney took his time answering. 'It's just an idea, Jim. I know damned well if I went into a bank a plumb stranger—an' wanted to walk out with a thousand dollars in cash for a piece of paper, they'd laugh me out of the building, unless I could prove the voucher warn't a forgery or maybe unless they knew me.'

The others gazed at Barney, who did not take his eyes off Jim Welsh. It was Pert Scovall who made a suggestion. 'I could figure on this better at the saloon.'

They trooped up there, Marshal Evans with them. The barman looked longest at Four Feathers. If he hadn't known him he would

48

have refused to serve him. It was the law; Indians were not allowed in saloons. It was against the law to sell them whiskey.

As they lined up the poker-faced saloonman brought bottles and glasses, hovered until it was clear they wanted nothing more from him then went to the far end of the bar where an old newspaper was spread, put on his glasses and ignored his customers.

Jim Welsh was quiet the longest. What Barney had intimated troubled him. He had known the Clarendon banker since Knowlton had arrived down there to take over the bank. He'd never had reason to think other than well of Knowlton. It bothered him now that Barney had made those insinuations about the banker. It bothered him more that Barney's reasoning had been convincing.

Win Evans, leaning on the bar with a loaded shot glass in one bony fist, said, 'Jim, you know that Knowlton-feller, you think he might have a hand in this rustlin' business?'

They all awaited Welsh's reply. It was slow coming and reluctantly given. 'I'll ride south and talk to him.'

The conversations continued for half an hour but Jim took no further part in it. There was something else: if Knowlton was involved with a gang of rustlers—what would prevent him from looting bank accounts, namely the account of Long Bow? It was an unsettling thought.

He rode back to the yard in stony silence which the men noticed. After the animals had been cared for and the men lounged at the barn, Jep said, 'Jim took that hard, Barney. I sure hope you're wrong.'

The oldest rangeman said, 'I hope so too, Jep. It was just somethin' that come to me.'

They went to the bunkhouse, fired up the stove and were in there acting like men who'd lost their last friend when Stub hit his horseshoes with the old hammer.

When they came out after eating there was a light in the main house. No one commented. At the bunkhouse they played pedro and talked. What bothered Pert Scovall was that they hadn't continued their pursuit of the rustlers. The other men played cards without pursuing what was obviously a foolish remark. They couldn't have caught them if they'd sprouted wings.

The following morning Jim left before sunup, which Stub commented on. No one told him where Jim was going. Ranch cooks were not usually included in subjects the riders believed were their private concerns.

In this case it did not bother Stub. He had the grandaddy of all headaches and the bottle in the flour barrel was down to the dregs.

Jep took them on a long ride up where the rustlers and Arapahos had tangled. They found brass casings, mostly from old guns, some dried blood and clear tracks heading in the direction of Lost River Valley, which they did not pursue; they already knew where the Indians had gone. They also knew which tribesmen it had been and were fairly well convinced why the broncos had been up in the trees on a dark night. To steal cattle.

They scouted around for about an hour then spread out to push cattle southward closer to the home place. It was an uneventful day until they were heading for the yard in mid-afternoon and Tad fell out of the saddle and landed face down without a sound.

The first man to swing off and roll him over was Barney. Jep came back, looked down and said, 'What the hell?' Four Feathers said, 'Fainted.'

It was Barney with an edge to his voice who put it in perspective. 'He's been doin' too much. Lend a hand gettin' him back on the horse.'

Tad recovered as they were settling him astraddle, looked around and said, 'What happened?'

Jep said, 'You fell off,' and went to his horse to mount. He and Barney rode on either side of Tad the remainder of the way to the yard. When they got there Tad swung off, led his horse into the barn to be stripped and took it out back to the corral where he was forking feed when Barney came, took away the hay fork and finished the feeding under Tad's baleful glare. 'I ain't crippled,' he exclaimed.

Barney went right on pitching feed when he replied, 'No one said you are, but you take it easy for a spell.'

Pert Scovall walked out back, saw the scowl on Tad's face, turned around and went back inside the barn.

Later, when Stub hit the horseshoes with his hammer and they had washed up, they headed for the cookshack. For some reason no one fathomed, Stub had spent most of the afternoon preparing a supper of roast beef cooked plumb through, mashed spuds and even some lemonade. After they had eaten he brought three pies made from wild apples. By that time the riders were stealing sideways glances at one another. Pert Scovall made one of his inane remarks. 'Your birthday, Stub?'

The cook blinked. 'Not that I know of. Why?'

Pert should have left the dead dog lying but he didn't. 'You never rassled up a supper like this since I been here.'

Stub walked to the table, fixed Pert with a withering glare and said, 'You're the best fed gang of wishbones of any outfit in this country. Always feed you like this—an' better.'

It was a blatant untruth but even tactless Pert Scovall let the matter die, at least until they were in the bunkhouse with the lamp lighted ready for their customary game of pedro, when Pert said, 'For a feller with a

52

disposition like a bear with a sore behind, Stub's one hell of a cook, when he wants to be, an' it's a fact he don't put out a meal like that even on Christmas.'

Jep looked at Scovall. 'You goin' to play cards or preach a sermon?'

The following morning when they trooped to the cookshack Stub was waiting. He fed all but Pert mounds of crisp fried spuds, toasted bread soggy with butter and strong coffee. Scovall got eggs as hard as boot-soles, half-burned potatoes and watered coffee.

They were at the barn with Pert grousing when Jim walked in, tired-looking but freshly scrubbed and shaved. He said, 'That's a long ride down an' back.'

They neither agreed nor disagreed. They stood like statues waiting for the rest of it. Jim sat on an overturned horseshoe keg. He did not mention the banker down at Clarendon. He said, 'Will Devon took his crew over to tear down that corral an' chute. Some old man came along with a shotgun and said if they touched that corral he'd shoot the lot of them. It turned out the old man owned the land an' let 'em build the corral because a feller with a black beard told him they only needed it once, then he could have it. The old man runs a few old gummer cows.'

Pert said, 'So they didn't tear it down.'

Jim ignored that. 'The old man told them it was late at night when he heard a steam engine. His shack isn't far off around a hill. He went outside, heard 'em loadin' cattle an' went back to bed.'

This time it was Jep who spoke. 'In the middle of the damned night he heard 'em loadin' cattle an' went back to bed?'

Jim nodded. 'Will told me that old squatter's been stealin' a critter off him now an' then since he took up his homestead. Will could never catch the old man nor find any hides off his butchered cattle. He said the old man lives alone, snarls at folks who come on to his land, an' as far as Will's concerned, is a disreputable old son of a bitch.'

When Jim resumed talking he still did not mention his ride down to Clarendon. He said, 'I stopped by the jailhouse on my way back. Win said the old woman who's taking care of Win's prisoner told him the feller's got blood poisoning.' That scrap of information held them all silent. No one survived blood poisoning.

'Win's going to question him for all he's worth before the feller starts driftin' off in the head.'

Jim arose from the little keg and finally said something they had been waiting to hear, but not the way they expected. 'Knowlton was not in Clarendon. His clerk said he'd gone to Denver on bank business. The liveryman told me he'd gone off in a buggy. No one drives all the way to Denver in a buggy, not when they can catch a train an' ride.'

No one spoke. Jim waited, and finally made one more revelation. 'Will Devon got his answer from the railroad people. Someone had hired an engine an' three cattle cars to go north to Laramie.'

Barney dryly said, 'Did they give Will a name?'

'Burton Moody.'

'They hired out their cars, just like that?' Jep asked.

Jim nodded his head. 'Railroads hire out, that's their business.'

'Did Moody give 'em an address?' Four Feathers asked.

Jim smiled thinly. 'Yeah. Fort Smith, Arkansas. Not real likely, is it?'

Pert disagreed. 'He could live there. I got a cousin in the chicken business lives in Fort Smith.'

Stub entered the barn to tell Jim a rider was coming from the south-east. They all went up as far as the front barn opening to watch. The horseman was approaching at a dead walk with loose reins. When he reached the barn and saw the men in the barn doorway, he swung off at the tie rack, looked around, visibly impressed, removed his gloves and said, 'Name's Ben Hobart. I was told at the town south-east of here an outfit called Long Bow lost some cattle to rustlers a few days back.'

Jim shoved out his hand and introduced

himself. Hobart was a sturdy man with reddish hair turning silver at the temples. He seemed to be one of those slow, deliberate people who did not get upset easily. That was confirmed when he said, 'I ranch ten miles south of Clarendon. I got raided about like I heard you got it; same way, stole cattle at night, drove 'em to a siding where they'd set up a chute, an' loaded 'em on a train.'

Jim invited Hobart to the main house. Barney took the stranger's horse inside to be cared for. Stub lingered but the riders headed for the bunkhouse. It was close enough to suppertime for Stub to get back to the cookshack so he did not go to the bunkhouse.

Jep and Barney went out back to wash up. While they were out there Jep said, 'These here cow thieves is about the slickest I ever heard of.'

Barney's retort was brusque. 'Not so damned slick they ain't goin' to end up on the end of a rope one of these days.'

Later, when the riders returned from supper there were two lamps burning at the main house. Barney made one of his dry remarks. 'They got a real good set of workin' corrals down at Clarendon. Why didn't them thieves use them instead of buildin' a corral an' a chute some miles below town?'

Jep's reply was given thoughtfully. 'Make too much noise loadin' cattle in town at night. I got to hand it to 'em. They got a real organized business goin'. When I was younger no one would ever have thought of usin' steam cars to rustle cattle.'

'In your day,' Barney said as he held the door for Jep to enter, 'they didn't have steam cars.'

5

AN UNEXPECTED TRIP

It turned out Ben Hobart ran a one-man cow outfit. Because one man couldn't handle over a couple of hundred head, his loss to the thieves—forty head—was enough to put him out of the ranching business. But he smiled, seemed relaxed and the Long Bow men liked him.

One thing they noticed after his fourth day at the bunkhouse was that his relaxed, loose manner was deceptive. When he roped or did the things stockmen traditionally did, his movements were quick and certain.

He smilingly accepted Jim's offer of hospitality because, he said, from what he'd been told Long Bow was doing something about rustlers other than talk. He told Jep he went by hunches, and his hunch at Long Bow was that eventually the rustlers would be caught and he wanted to be around when that happened, a perfectly understandable thing to say by someone who had been seriously injured by thieves.

When Jim went to see Marshal Evans he took Hobart along. The lawman acknowledged their introduction with a handclasp and an unsmiling expression. After he had heard about Hobart's loss Win Evans took them to the saloon where it was as cool inside as the beer. When the marshal said he was supposed to meet Will Devon directly, they parted, but when Jim went to his horse to mount, Win followed. While Jim was snugging up the cinch he had loosened earlier, Win said, 'You know who that feller is?'

Jim turned, considered the lawman's solemn expression and shook his head. 'No.'

'You remember six, seven years ago there was a shoot-out down at Timville about thirty miles south of Clarendon?'

Jim nodded. Years back that fight had been the highlight of local interest for a long time. Three men shot it out with seventeen Mexican border-jumpers. When the smoke cleared six border-jumpers were dead, and one of their opponents was alive.

Jim said, 'What about it?'

As was his custom the marshal spoke in a punctuated drawl. 'I thought I'd seen him somewhere . . . it come to me at the jailhouse when he was talkin' . . . that's the feller who come out alive. Ben Hobart . . . I heard he took up some land and set up a ranch.'

Jim looked down the tie rack where Hobart was swinging into the saddle. He said, 'Are you sure?'

Win frowned faintly. 'I remember the red hair an' the sort of easy-goin' way he had. I met him twice down at Clarendon . . . they told me down there who he was.'

The marshal let that soak in before speaking again on a different subject. 'That feller who calls himself Abe Lincoln . . . he's dyin' of blood poisonin'. The midwife told me he'd die sure as hell so I went an' had a long talk with him. He told me Moody's got a partner . . . in the rustlin' business. He didn't know anythin' more'n that. But he did tell me Moody's takin' his operation westerly.'

'Where, westerly?'

'He didn't know. All he knew was that him an' the other fellers was to meet him at a place called Kingsville . . . you ever heard of Kingsville?'

Jim hadn't. 'No.'

Evans said, 'I'll find out where it is. It come to me while I was feedin' him whiskey to keep him talkin' . . . that if we could find out where Kingsville is . . . an' providin' they ain't been already raided over there . . . we could maybe get over there an' catch the sons of bitches.'

Jim mounted, evened up his reins and looked down. 'When you find out, let me know.'

Marshal Evans watched Ben Hobart ride up to join Jim and watched the pair of them head north-west for home. He went down to his jailhouse, ignored the short, rasping sounds of his prisoner, dug around until he found a map of the territory and after fifteen minutes of walking his finger from bottom to near the top of the westerly country, located Kingsville.

It appeared as little more than a well and peach tree at the side of a crooked roadway running north to south. He sat down, scratched, used his finger to trace out something else—a railroad symbol which paralleled Kingsville but what he had to guess was a short distance east where the country was not so rugged.

He stowed the map, looked in on his prisoner briefly and was heading for the doorway when the midwife came to look at her patient. Win went back with her and stood in the cell's doorway as the woman leaned to consider Abe Lincoln. When she finished her examination she came to the door to say, 'This'll be the second Abe Lincoln cut off in his prime. He won't last another day. Want me to tell the carpenter?'

Win shook his head. 'Not until he's dead,' he said, and followed the woman out into bright sunlight. This time he did not bother locking the jailhouse. Even if Abe Lincoln had friends and they came for him, all they'd get would be either a dead man or one close to it.

Over at the general store Win took advantage of a slack time to engage Sam Ewart in a seemingly casual conversation, but Sam had never heard of a place called Kingsville except for a town back in Missouri, nor did he recollect ever doing business with a man who dressed in city clothes named Moody.

Win struck gold by accident on his way north to the stage company's corralyard when the toothless, string-bean of a saddle- and harness-maker came out to address Win as the marshal was passing. 'Ever seen such a fine day?' the wiry old gummer asked, and made an exaggerated effort at deep breathing which immediately brought a brief fit of coughing.

Win waited, then said, 'It's them Mex stogies, Homer.'

The harness-maker stopped admiring the day. 'Like hell. It's the ragweed. Every blessed summer when it's bloomin' I cough. Years back when I worked for a feller near the Utah border an' I'd get to coughin', he told me what it was because he had the same trouble.'

'Over near the Utah line?'

'Yes. For three years. He was as good a leatherman as ever lived. He could—'

'What town, Homer?'

'Place called Fort Drum.'

Win remembered his finger passing over a town by that name. He said, 'You know of a place called Kingsville over there?'

The harness-maker nodded. 'Sure. It's about the size of most of them Mormon villages over into Utah.'

'Cattle country, Homer?'

'That's all the Kingsville country is fit for. The country over into Utah too, for that matter.'

'They got a railroad siding at Kingsville?'

'Yes, but you come to Leesville first. It's too small for a way station. You got to go north a piece to reach Kingsville.'

'They got a telegraph, Homer?'

'Fort Drum? I just told you it ain't no more'n a wide place on the wagon trail.'

'They got a lawman?'

The harness-maker cocked his head. 'You got an interest in that country, Win? Let me tell you, to make a livin' over there you got to put on a tin beak an' get down'n scratch with the chickens.'

After Marshal Evans left the old gummer he turned back, walked down to the livery barn, told the dayman to bring in his horse, and rode mostly west and a tad north, and noticed for a fact it was indeed a magnificent day, the sky was as clear as glass, it was warm without being hot and visibility was so good if a man stood in his stirrups he could have seen tomorrow.

When he reached Long Bow's yard only the cook was there. He told the marshal Jim had gone out with the crew. They were pushing cattle away from the distant hills and therefore probably wouldn't be back until suppertime.

Win asked about Ben Hobart. Stub wrinkled his nose. 'He's with 'em. Jim's got a bad habit of puttin' up strangers.'

The ride was wasted time. He could not wait until evening so he left a note with Stub for Jim to come see him as soon as he could, and returned to town just in time to be one of the last diners before the caféman locked up for the night.

At the jailhouse there was a two-wheeled handcart out front. Inside two townsmen and the town carpenter were rolling Abe Lincoln in a soiled old length of canvas. The midwife was standing aside. When Win walked in the men lifted their bundle and started past. They nodded to the marshal but did not say a word. The midwife did though. 'I came by but he was dead. Fifty, Marshal, he warn't old enough to die, but I expect if a man chooses that way of makin' a livin' he'll go young, by shootin', hangin', or the way this one went. Did he have any kin?'

Win answered as he twisted to watch the corpse being loaded into the carpenter's cart. 'I got no idea . . . all I know is that he said his name was Abe Lincoln, an' that was a damned lie.'

The midwife looked outside too as she said, 'Maybe not, Mister Evans. One time when I was a girl I paid a nickel to see a tall shrivelled-up corpse the feller—a travellin' snake-oil peddlers—wore in front of a crowd was President Lincoln; that he'd been dug up an' sold to the peddler.'

Win gazed at the midwife, nodded. He lighted a lamp and sat down and brought out the map and opened it on his desk. He was trying to guess just how far it was to Leesville when Jim Welsh walked in, dusty and tired. He sank down on a chair and said, 'Stub gave me the note. We got back about an hour after you left . . . what's on the map?'

Win ran his finger down to Leesville and said, 'Look . . . I figure it's about a hunnert an' fifty miles . . . maybe two hunnert miles from here to there. Another mile or two to Kingsville.'

Jim leaned over the map as he said, 'And if we make a run for it we might get over there after the rustlers made their raid.'

Marshal Evans rocked back in his chair. Before he could speak Jim asked a question. 'Did Abe Lincoln say when they were all to meet over there?'

Evans shook his head. 'No . . . but I been thinkin', after the Devon raid, and considerin' how far it is from here to Leesville an' how long it'd take 'em all to get over there, we might make it in time. An' we might not . . . but one thing's a cinch, talkin' an' settin' around here'll sure-Lord decrease our chances of gettin' over there in time. What do you think?'

Jim straightened up and returned to his

64

chair. 'I'll bring in the crew in the morning. It'll kill a day ridin' down to Clarendon to get a train that'll get us over there. How about you? There's no way of telling how long this'll take an' you got your job around town.'

The marshal rocked back again gazing pensively at the map. 'It don't seem to me that folks won't understand. Even folks in town is roiled up over both you'n Will Devon gettin' raided. For all I know them bastards could come back and raid again . . . I'll explain things to Sam across the road . . . he can tell around town why I won't be around for a spell.'

Jim continued to relax in the chair for a short while before rising. 'It'll depend on timing, Win, an' after we get over there we'll need horses. My guess is that a place no bigger'n Leesville won't have a livery barn.'

'We could get a cattle car an' take our own animals, couldn't we?'

Jim stood by the door without opening it. Eventually he made a mirthless small smile. 'Not if they've already raided before we get over there.' He looked at the seated lawman. 'All right, I'll see you in the morning with the crew.'

'And Mister Hobart?'

'If he wants to come along.'

Evans was rising when he said, 'He will.'

Jim had used a fresh horse to reach town, so he loped part of the way back. Even so the crew had eaten and were at their game of pedro when he arrived in the yard.

They sat at the scarred old bunkhouse table as silent as stones when Jim walked in, got himself a cup of coffee, sat down and related what he and Win Evans had decided. Afterwards the only rider who had an immediate response was Pert Scovall. He said, 'Suppose they already raided over there at Fort Drum or Kingsville?'

Jim was too tired to say why he and the marshal felt there was to be a raid, he simply said, 'We take chances every day, Pert. We're taking one now.'

Ben Hobart was smoking a little pipe which he removed to say he'd like to go along. Jim nodded. 'It's up to you. How long can you be away from home?'

'Oh, I got a good woman an' a half-grown boy. They'll make out fine. Mainly, I want to meet up with the fellers who stole close to a one fifth of my cattle.'

Jim went back to the main house, bedded down and slept like a log. At the bunkhouse there was conversation right up to the moment Stub walked in after cleaning up after supper and setting dough to rise for bread for the next day.

Stub picked up on what was being said, and volunteered to go along. After an awkward silence Jep told him it was customary for someone to be in the yard, something the cook knew. For days on end, particularly during the seasons when cattle were being worked, he was the only Long Bow man at the home place. He did not argue, which relieved the rangeboss, who did not like arguing—or playing cards—with the cook.

The men finished their card game, got out their weapons to be sure they were clean and working, sat a while discussing what might happen then turned in.

It was a moonless night, the kind even wolves did not prefer but to bears it made little difference. They would have to go a long way to find the cattle which were no longer near the timbered uplands, a greater distance than bears would go unless they were very hungry.

Stub surprised everyone. It was still as dark as the inside of a well when he vigorously beat his horseshoes. He had been up and stirring an hour and a half. When the riders were jarred awake by the racket, someone spoke in the dark. 'What'n hell got that old screwt up in the middle of the damned night?'

Barney replied dryly, 'His conscience.'

By the time they got to the cookhouse with its lighted lanterns Stub was ready to feed them. Tad looked sullenly at the cook. 'It's only a little past midnight.'

Stub smiled. 'You boys is goin' on a long ride. I figured to feed you hearty. Besides, there's been a light at the main house since I got over here.'

He did indeed feed them well, steak and

spuds, all the coffee they wanted, sourdough biscuits light as a feather covered with pepper-gravy, and bread so fresh it was still warm.

When they were over at the barn Four Feathers said, 'I'm gettin' to almost like Stub.'

None of the others would go that far but for a fact they had enjoyed the meal.

Jim appeared, nodded around, brought in a horse, rigged it and led it out front to be mounted. As the others did the same Jim said, 'Win'll be waiting at the livery barn,' and led off in a stiff walk, to which he held for a mile until the horses were 'warmed out' then rode at a lope.

The sky had stars, otherwise it was as black as soot. There hadn't been a moon nor did visibility improve much even after they reached town.

Marshal Evans hadn't eaten for two excellent reasons, he was not married and the caféman would not fire up his stove for another couple of hours. He was chewing pemmican when the Long Bow men arrived. A few grunted greetings were exchanged before Marshal Evans got his rigged-out horse from a stall, led it out front and the livery barn nighthawk came out to watch them ride southward, hugging himself inside a ragged old blanketcoat.

It was cold; the riders rode coated and gloved. By Barney's estimate they would reach Clarendon by late afternoon and their animals would be tired when they got down there.

Tad, who was riding stirrup with the older man, rolled and lighted a smoke. Barney looked around. 'Them things ain't good for you,' he said.

Tad's reply was swift. 'Neither's ridin' in the damned cold on a night so dark a man can hardly see the ears of his horse. Barney, chewin'll rot your innards, didn't you know that?'

The conversation ended. Up ahead Jim and Win Evans exchanged a wink. Most men were cranky early in the morning even after a good breakfast, and the older they got the crankier they got. Riding in the darkness and the cold made them even more cantankerous. Sunshine and warmth would change that but for as long as it remained dark and cold Barney was testy.

After sunrise they got to the edge of the road for a stage and four to pass, otherwise, excepting a sod-buster with a wagon loaded with farm-raised vegetables also heading south, they did not meet any traffic.

They halted twice to loosen cinches and rest the animals. The last time they did this Tad Butler fell asleep. When Barney roused him the older man looked worried. As Tad was snugging up Barney said, 'You feel all right? You look a mite peaked.'

Tad was annoyed. 'I feel fine an' how can you tell I look peaked in the dark?'

It hadn't been dark for several hours but

Barney offered no reply.

When they had rooftops in sight it was mid-afternoon. By the time they entered Clarendon the sun was well down with shadows forming.

Win left the others seeking the Clarendon town marshal with whom he briefly visited, then hiked to the railroad building. Over there they told him there would be an engine along in a couple of hours to unload some pure-bred cows for a local cowman and he could load his horses in that car. They also told him the train would reach Leesville by late the following night, that it would have arrived earlier but it had been ordered by telegraph from the main office in Denver to take on an extra pair of cattle cars for use up north at Kingsville.

While they waited for their engine and car Barney asked Jim if those cars to be used might not be needed by rustlers.

The idea intrigued them all. Pert Scovall said, 'Suppose we're goin' west an' them rustlers is goin' east with stolen cattle an' we pass 'em. What do we do then?'

The others gazed at Pert without speaking. There was only one set of tracks.

8

THE TRAIN

Their train had no passenger car. It had six box cars, presumably loaded with industrial or mercantile items. The Long Bow men rode in the last car, a caboose which had a small iron stove. Trainmen came and went. The Long Bow men nodded to them but remained apart, which did not appear to bother the trainmen who, for the most part, used several bunks. Jim thought the trainmen, while affable when they could not avoid it, considered themselves professionals, apart from stockmen.

At their second stop where the engine sent up gusts of white steam, the trainmen pulled down a large spout and refilled the water reservoir. Jim asked how long they would stop at this place and the trainman answered curtly, as he guided the large pipe into its hole, yelling over the sounds made by the engine, 'Fifteen minutes. If you are figurin' to stretch your legs I wouldn't go far.'

Jim said, 'We need feed and water for the horses.'

The trainman answered as he was bracing against the water pipe, 'In a couple of hours we'll stop at a place called Boone's Well. Most likely you can buy feed. It'll be along toward daylight. You can get water at the station.' That trainman did not appear in the caboose so Jim surmised he probably worked up front nearer the engine.

One trainman made a pot of coffee on the little iron stove and offered cups around. All the Long Bow men thanked him and drank coffee, which was never a good substitute for food but it beat hell out of a snow bank.

Four Feathers slept, Pert Scovall did too, and his snoring was audible above most of the noises of the train. Ben Hobart sat, feet propped up, hat tipped back, whittling, quiet enough to give the impression he was a long way off in his thoughts. Barney and Tad sat near windows. It was impossible to make things out as they passed unless they were close to the tracks. When they passed two villages without stopping Jim frowned but said nothing.

By the time they reached Boone's Well dawn had arrived and visibility was fair. The train halted beside a high platform, someone up ahead noisily slid open a heavy door and the sound of men's voices brought all the Long Bow men except Pert and the 'breed to the little railed landing below which there were steel steps.

Win Evans said, 'Off-loadin'. Looks like we got time . . . to find horse feed.'

The station master wore dark sleeve garters from wrist to elbow, a blue eyeshade, probably out of habit because the sun hadn't appeared yet. He nodded briskly at the Long Bow men. He already knew who they were and what their destination was. Telegraph lines ran both ways near the train tracks. When Jim asked about horse feed the stationman had a pat answer ready. 'Outside, near the end of the platform. Buckets too. There's a pipe down there.' At Jim's bewildered look the man with the blue eyeshade smiled smugly. 'We was telegraphed ahead from Clarendon. You can settle up with the station master back there.'

They went to the dark unlighted part of the platform and sure enough there were stacked buckets and a tidy stock of timothy hay with just enough Dutch clover in it to smell pleasant.

Four Feathers and Pert appeared, puffy-eyed but alert. Each of them took his place in the bucket brigade while Jim, Ben Hobart and Win Evans pitched hay. It was the kind of work that brought men wide awake and kept them that way. It also got their blood flowing which was fortunate because Colorado pre-mornings are cold.

They finished their chores and were back in the warm caboose before the Boone's Well freight was stacked on the platform.

The horses had been cared for which left one problem—none of the men had eaten in quite a spell.

When a trainman came out of the cold grey

dawn they asked him about food. He was a large, bull-built man with the eyes of a ferret and an authoritative manner, he barely answered as he headed for one of the bunks. 'If you ride a freight train, boys, you either bring your food or you go hungry.'

The large man's attitude as well as his answer did not sit well. Barney said, 'You fellers don't eat on the train?'

The large man stopped to look down where Barney was sitting. 'We eat, mister. See them two high cupboards with locks on 'em? We load 'em for long hauls.'

Barney, Tad and Four Feathers gazed at the cabinets whose large brass padlocks swayed with the train's movement. Ben Hobart closed his clasp knife, rose pocketing it, went over to examine the padlocks and with a blur of movement drew his six-gun and shot off both locks. The noise was thunderous.

The startled large trainman came up off his bunk like he had been lying on a spring. He let out a roar and started for Hobart. Four Feathers shoved out a foot. The trainman went down in cursing sprawl. When he got up on all fours to jump to his feet Win Evans leaned, pushed a six-gun into the man's face and cocked it.

The train's slight rocking and multiple noises were clearly audible in the caboose as the trainman remained on all fours like a gut-shot bear. Win gestured with the cocked gun.

'Go back to bed an' stay there.'

The trainman who'd had fight in him when he'd jumped up from the bunk, had no fight in him now. The bravest soul on earth was likely to suffer from genuine fear when a cocked pistol was six inches from his face and the man holding it showed cold resolve in his eyes.

The cupboards were well stocked. Ben Hobart handed out tins of fruit, vegetables and bullybeef—too salty for most palates unless it was boiled—but not to hungry men riding a train through a brightening morning.

An hour later, with the food locker pretty well emptied the trainman sat up. The Long Bow men ignored him until he rose, then Barney said, 'Sit down, mister, an' stay down.'

The large man sat on the edge of the bunk, quiet for as long as it took him to study each one of them, then he spoke to the man with a badge on his vest. 'You're going to be in a heap of trouble when we reach Kingsville.' To which Marshal Evans quietly replied, 'Mister, my business is trouble. Rest easy . . . you'll be paid for the vittles . . . and for the busted cupboards.' The marshal then said, 'We didn't have no choice.'

The trainman, emboldened, replied sharply, 'Why didn't you bring your own grub? Us fellers who work on the trains do an—'

Four Feathers spoke. 'Mister, I never been on steam cars before. How about you Barney?'

'Nope, never have, an' can tell you right

here'n now I don't favour 'em. Except for your damned steam cars we wouldn't be here.'

The trainman subsided. The men facing him were not exactly hostile but they certainly were—different. He leaned back and watched the sunlit countryside go by.

Jim slept. Only Ben Hobart, back whittling, his feet cocked, remained awake. The train shunted to stop at two villages before the sun was overhead. At both places water was taken from a high wooden tower then the train continued on its way. Jim thought the train's direction had been slanting around northward somewhat. He asked the trainman how far they were from Kingsville.

The large man answered sullenly. 'A fair distance. We'll get there about sundown, maybe an hour before.'

Win Evans had a question for the trainman. 'Do we stop at Leesville?'

'Only for water. There's nothin' there but a store and some shacks.'

The Long Bow men palavered. Because of what they'd heard, about the engine with cattle cars being sent to Kingsville, they had intended to leave the train at Leesville.

Something about this bothered Barney. He went back to ask the trainman some questions. One of them was did the trainman know if a train pulling empty cattle cars had gone ahead of them. The trainman's answer deepened the mystery for Barney. He said, 'There hasn't been a train go north from Clarendon in a week . . . maybe more'n likely two weeks.'

'Well then, is there a train with cattle cars follerin' behind us?'

The trainman considered Barney as though he were talking to a child. 'Mister, this here is the only set of cars goin' north, an' no set of cars is following us. You know why?'

Barney shook his head. 'No.'

'Because there's only one set of tracks, that's why. If there was a set of cars coming east we'd have to stop. There aren't any sidings between where we are now and Kingsville; an' Denver, which controls all trains, wouldn't have none following. You see?'

Barney said, 'Thanks', and went back to the rear of the caboose to tell his companions what the trainman had said. As the others considered this Pert Scovall spoke up. 'I'll tell you somethin'. I've seen trains go in reverse for one hell of a distance.' At the annoyed look Pert got he spoke a little louder. 'Suppose them rustlers loaded up at Kingsville and run their engine backward all the way to Wyoming? Trains go backwards as good as they go forward.'

Again the others considered Pert, but this time Win Evans went back where the trainman was and asked him if trains ran backwards. The trainman's gaze at Win was almost pitying. 'They run backward as good as they

77

run forward. Why?'

Win did not reply, he returned to the rear of the caboose and said, 'If the cars them thieves use come south, maybe from up in Wyoming, after they loaded the rustled beef the train could run backwards all the way back from where it come from.'

For a long time there was no further conversation. Not until, with the sun sloping away, the trainman rose and said, 'I got to pee.'

Win nodded at the man. 'Go ahead,' and smiled enigmatically because he knew the trainman would not return, but would go up through the cars to warn his fellow trainmen about the stockmen in the caboose.

Four Feathers did not like that. 'They'll come back here loaded for bear.'

Tad did not think so. 'If I ever saw anyone who most likely never owned a gun, an' sure-Lord don't wear guns, it's the fellers who unloaded that freight back yonder.' Then Tad shrugged. 'Anyway, we're so close now all we got to do is talk their ears off then leave the cars at Leesville.'

It didn't quite come off like that. They had a village's rooftops in sight when they were jarred off balance to the accompaniment of hissing steam as the train came to a lunging halt. Through the sound of escaping steam they heard men running down the far side of the cars. Pert looked out and swore. 'Hell.

78

They're comin' an' one's got a shotgun. Two others got pistols.'

Win and Ben Hobart peeked out. Ben Hobart drew back to shake his head. 'They're all on the east side.'

Win stepped across the iron rear of the caboose and peeked. Hobart was right, all the irate trainmen were on the east side. Clearly, the situation was new to them. If it hadn't been they'd have split up and approached the caboose from both sides.

Jim went to look and one of the hurrying trainmen saw him and yelled. Jim pulled back, palmed his six-gun, knelt to ease out for another look, saw the nearest man with a scattergun and fired at the ground in front, which made the shotgun-bearer leap into the air and turn as though to retreat but the large trainman behind him gave the shotgun-man a hard punch, cursed him and pushed him back around. But that alone could not overcome the shotgun-man's terror. He took root where he stood, the other trainmen passed on both sides of him.

Win Evans stepped into full view on the side of the platform without a gun in his hand. The foremost trainman wore a round hat with a shiny visor. He was holding a carbine. Behind him was the large man the Long Bow men had kept in the caboose. He said something indistinguishable to the man in the dark matching coat and britches who wore the

79

visored hat, and that individual stopped in his tracks looking up. He made no move to use his carbine.

Win addressed that man. 'Mister, we're goin' to unload at Leesville. We don't want no trouble—unless you force it.'

The large trainman growled again but the man with the round hat told him to shut up. He then regarded Win as he said, 'You got a right to that badge, mister?'

Evans nodded. 'I'm town marshal at Cedarville. You know where that is?'

The jowly man with the visored hat nodded without speaking.

Win stood with thumbs hooked in his belt. 'We're after cattle thieves. They're likely somewhere around Leesville or Kingsville. Now then, you want to haul us the rest of the way to Leesville or not?'

The jowly man stood a long moment, expressionless and unmoving. When the large man muttered behind him he turned to loudly say, 'We'll take 'em to Leesville. Bill, you ride up front, stay away from the caboose.'

As Win started to thank the jowly man that individual turned his back and using his carbine waved to someone far ahead.

The engine stopped emitting steam. The trainmen scurried for steps, the last to go was the man with the visored hat. He looked up at Win Evans. 'Who told you there was rustlers around Leesville?'

Jim answered from an open window. 'We're playin' a hunch. It's a gamble.'

'An' if you're wrong, mister?'

'We'll have a long ride home,' Jim answered as the jowly man moved close, caught a handrail and disappeared into the moving train.

Win Evans sat down opposite Jim Welsh and blew out a relieved breath without speaking. As the train gathered momentum Pert Scovall said, 'Where's Feathers?'

They looked, did not find the 'breed and Tad said, 'While the marshal was talkin' to fatface Feathers went down the far side of the cars. He told me he wanted to get in with the horses.'

Barney said irritably, 'What in hell for?'

Tad answered his roping partner just as irritably. 'To be handy with his Winchester if a fight started—why else?'

The train never gathered full momentum before it let off steam and began to lose headway. Pert leaned out and called back, 'If this is Leesville Gen'l Lee wouldn't think much of it.'

He was right, General Lee wouldn't have. Leesville had what appeared to be one store with a scattering of log houses interspersed with tarpaper shacks. The place had not been laid out with any sense of order. Most likely, as with other places of the same size, it had come into existence because there was water, with some of the most uninviting range country a man could imagine on all sides.

Unloading the horses required a ramp which the trainmen grudgingly put into place with the help of the Long Bow riders. Because by this time there was little amiability on either side, as the Long Bow men led their horses clear of the tracks to be saddled and bridled there was no exchange of waved salutes.

Four Feathers mounted near Jim, squinted and said, 'I don't see no corrals.'

There were no corrals. In fact there was no siding for cars to park while being loaded. No corrals and no chutes.

Jim led off in the direction of the town, where several curious onlookers had watched the train depart, and as it did there was a band of horsemen waiting for the last car to clear the way before riding toward the village.

Leesville's storekeeper was also the saloonman. The two businesses were kept separate by a large wagon canvas on which someone had painted what was supposed to be a nice blue-water creek with improbably high trees in the background. He was a shrew of a man, wispy-haired, unshaven and with the variety of long nose that people in Texas would have said reminded them of Davy Crockett.

He was also unctuous; that many armed men filing into his store behoved him to be. None of the strangers smiled, one wore a badge and there was a 'breed Indian wearing his best imitation of the expression of a scalp-hunter.

Jim asked about food. The sparrow-built, darkly weathered man said there was no eatery but he could supply plenty of tinned peaches and whatnot.

The men from Cedarville browsed among the shelves taking what they wanted. The storekeeper tried to watch them as Jim asked questions. The first one was about a corral and loading chute in the area which was probably new and had been built beside the railroad tracks.

The wispy man knew of no such things but a threadbare old man who looked like he had an aversion to soap and water who had come to lean in the doorway with several other locals, said, 'You got a reason for askin', mister?'

All the strangers stopped what they had been doing to turn as Jim said, 'We're trying to find the gents who built those things, and a feller named Moody.'

The unwashed, thin, older man said, 'Burt Moody?' and all the strangers froze.

Jim said, 'Burt Moody. You know him?'

The old man, noticing two things, the badge on the shirt of one of the strangers, and the abrupt cessation of movement among the strangers, replied quietly. 'Yeah, I know him. He give me a horse to guide him around the country some time back.'

'How far back?' Jim asked.

'About a month. He's a cattle buyer. He wanted to look over the stock in our country before he went among the ranchers to maybe start buyin'.'

This was making Barney impatient. With the exception of Win Evans people who drawled and took forever to say things annoyed him. He said, 'Where is Moody now—do you know?'

The old man put his attention upon the other older man. 'I ain't sure. He never come back after we rode all over the territory. I figured he'd seen all he wanted to see. He give me a nice horse, got a little age on him but what the hell, so have I. I'd say if you gents want to find him you might go up to Kingsville. They got eateries an' a hotel up there.'

Jim handed the old man a silver dollar. The other men near the doorway watched this and one of them addressed the storekeeper. 'Is the bar open now, Gordon?'

The storekeeper forced a smile and a nervous giggle when he replied, 'It's open. Give me time to settle up with these gents an' I'll be in there.'

Jim paid the storekeeper, who counted every coin as they were placed on his counter, then beamed. 'If you boys is comin' back this way, stop by.'

Jim nodded, no one else did, and the men from the Long Bow with Ben Hobart and Win Evans, walked out into the dying day with their

84

tins of peaches, a rangeman's delight, sacks of tobacco, a few plugs for those who chewed, flat tins of sardines, something rangemen could carry in shirt pockets without causing a bulge, and candy, enough licorice root and other sweets to last a long time.

Dusk was closing in. They rode west of Leesville until they found good grass and a creek, cared for their animals and built a small fire. Because they had no utensils to cook with they ate straight from the opened tins. When they finished Jim said, 'In the morning if we spread far out an' ride both sides of the railroad track towards Kingsville maybe we'll find something. Maybe a corral an' a loading chute.'

7

HEADING NORTH

Jim's surmise was wrong. They rode parallel to the tracks the full distance to Kingsville and found no corral or chute. With Kingsville in sight Pert stood in his stirrups as he said, 'Now there's a town a man can get fed in an' maybe have somethin' to drink.'

Considering the distance it was a good guess. Kingsville—named by a rarity among the old hide-hunters, an educated man—was called after the royal head of the country the hunter had come from—Prussia. But that story had almost been lost over time, and the place had grown since then. It not only had four saloons, one church and two cafés, it even had a bank, big sycamore trees lining Main Street, a stage company and a livery barn. The latest addition had been an apothecary.

Because of the railroad Kingsville had mushroomed with promise that it would continue to expand; even the jailhouse had been rebuilt.

Jim led his riders past the east side of town northward. When Ben Hobart said, 'They got corrals an' chutes.' Jim nodded and kept on riding. He wanted to be assured there were none of those trademarks of the Moody outfit farther north. They would turn back after they were certain none of those other corrals had been constructed, but from what he and Will Devon had decided, the cow thieves stayed clear of towns, made their loading corrals some distance away, as they had done back at Clarendon.

It was discouraging to spend an entire day hunting for something they did not find. When they turned back with the sun gone, they had Kingsville's lights to guide them, and for a fact after dark the town seemed even larger than it was. Outlying structures formed an uneven, mostly random, set of lights.

The liveryman paid no appreciable

attention to so many strangers arriving in a group. It either had happened before or the liveryman only cared that business should be so good. He was a burly, bearded, taciturn man with two fingers off his left hand. When Jim asked about a rooming-house the man pointed with his right hand. 'Up yonder—you see that green light? Lady that runs it keeps a green light in the parlour next to the winder when she's got empty rooms, which is most of the time.'

They crossed to the nearest café, walked in and the caféman's jaw dropped. He was surprised to see so many strangers enter his eatery in one group. He was not entirely pleased because in half an hour he closed up for the day and feeding this bunch was going to take more than a half-hour.

He got their coffee first, told them he had either antelope steaks or venison backstrap, they could take their pick.

They unanimously ordered antelope. They also asked him to leave the coffee pot on the counter, which he did, and told him they wanted potatoes, gravy and bread to sop up the gravy with.

His only other customers were two men, one older, one younger. Although they nodded they concentrated on their supper until the older man looked up and addressed Marshal Evans. 'You likely don't remember but I rode in a couple of posses with you when I lived over at Cedarville.'

Win's brows drew together. The man looked familiar but that was all. They were both rangemen from their looks. The older man also said, somewhat dryly, 'I'd take off that badge if I was you.'

Win moved to take the badge off as he said, 'Why?'

'Well,' the older rangeman said, 'for one thing it don't mean anythin' this far from Cedarville. For another thing, Mister Hogan, Kingsville's constable, is touchy about things like that.'

The younger rider spoke for the first time, grinning a little as he said, 'Mister Hogan's touchy about everything.'

When the food arrived, the pair of local rangemen arose to depart. As the older one passed he slapped Win lightly on the shoulder. 'Good to see you again,' he said, and followed his companion out into the night.

The caféman's curiosity had been increasing steadily as he heard what the local rangemen had said. He hovered over his only other customers like a mother hen. When Barney pointed to the pie table in back and asked what kind of pie the caféman had, the answer came back swiftly. 'Rhubarb'n sour apple.'

Barney nodded and went back to sopping gravy with bits of bread. The caféman still hovered. 'Which one you want?'

Barney replied around a mouthful. 'Neither.

I never could stomach rhubarb an' sour apples ain't much better.'

Tad, beside Barney, piped up, 'I'll take a piece of that sour-apple pie.'

They cleaned their plates down to the china, killed fifteen minutes with coffee, then asked the caféman what time he opened in the morning. The answer was five o'clock—it really was an hour later but these strangers cleaned their plates and there were a lot of them. Business was business; a man knew about options and this was one of them.

The woman at the rooming-house was different than the caféman and the liveryman. She needed business but not so many at one time particularly not after sundown which was her private supper and knitting time. She did not smile as she led the men inside to rooms.

She only had one rule of the house; no drinking in the rooms. Pert groaned, the others, including the landlady, ignored that. As she stood aside for Jim and Win to enter one of the rooms she also said, 'The back winders is nailed closed,' and walked away leaving them to figure that one out.

They slept like the dead. The last twenty-four hours had been bearable but not particularly pleasant. On full stomachs, tired to the bone a cannon might have awakened them but nothing less would have.

They didn't make it down to the café until six o'clock but the proprietor, who had been up earlier, welcomed them with hot coffee and an unctuous smile. There were four or five other diners, unmarried men who worked in town, who paid little attention to the Long Bow strangers.

They did not dawdle after breakfast but went down to the livery barn for their animals. The liveryman, never amiable so early in the morning, helped with the saddling and bridling but did not even go up front to watch the strangers ride out of town.

They were noticed; most businesses were open for customers. The saloons were still locked tight, otherwise Kingsville was preparing for another day and while roadway traffic would be brisk later, this early what looked like a band of strangers—and hard-riders at that—started the inevitable speculation.

By the time Constable Jim Hogan heard enough to be interested the Long Bow men, with Ben Hobart and Win Evans, were about a mile northward picking up the train tracks where they had left off the evening before.

They rode without haste on both sides of the tracks. By midday they had found no corral or loading chute but they came upon some track workers with their sidecar at hand upon which were the tools and new ties which were to replace several ties that had rotted.

The foreman was a muscular Irishman with a snub nose, merry pale eyes and a pair of hands half the size of a small ham.

When he and the other labourers saw the riders approaching on both sides of the tracks they stopped working and leaned on their crowbars and shovels to watch.

Jim nodded to the Irishman, introduced himself and asked questions which the Irishman answered without hesitation. Yes, he told Jim, there had been a corral and chute at track side another couple of miles north, but they had been dismantled. The Irishman had no idea when or why, he had last seen them several weeks earlier, but when he came south from Borderton to patch track this morning, the corral and chute were gone. 'An' no sign of 'em,' the Irishman said. 'No logs or posts left. Whoever done it cleaned up afterwards, somethin' you don't see often.'

They rode north, found where post holes had been partially filled in, rode back to Kingsville and hunted up the station master, another of those dedicated individuals who wore an eyeshade and black sleeve protectors from wrist to elbow, which made Barney begin to wonder if those things weren't some kind of railroad uniform.

Jim leaned on the counter behind which was the telegraph apparatus, some chairs and a cluttered desk. The station master eyed the weathered, rumpled men who entered his office, filling it, and apprehensively went to lean on the counter and smile.

Jim Welsh nodded but offered no greeting.

He said, 'You know a place some miles north of town where cattle was loaded not too long ago?'

The station master inclined his head. 'Yes, sir. It was some fellers who drove cattle from down south an' was takin' them up to Wyoming. Two of 'em come to see me to explain why they didn't want to use our local corrals and chutes.'

'Why didn't they?' Jep asked, leaning beside Jim.

'The critters had hoof-and-mouth disease. I was grateful for bein' told that. Hoof-and-mouth is real catchin'. If it got started in our area cattle'd die like flies.'

Jim and Win exchanged a glance. The marshal used his most amiable tone when he addressed the station master. 'Where in Wyomin' did they take the cattle?'

'They never said an' I never asked. All's I done was arrange for two cattle cars to come down from Borderton, take the cattle on board and get 'em the hell out of this country. That sickness spreads like wildfire.'

'Do any of the local cowmen know about them cattle?' Barney asked. The station master vigorously shook his head. 'No, an' you gents would do us all a favour if you never mentioned it once you walk out of here.'

Jim said, 'Not a word, friend, if you'll give us the name of the feller who told you about the *aftosa* an' what the destination of those cattle was.'

The station master returned to his desk, sifted through its disarray until he found a piece of paper and brought it back to the counter with him. He reversed it and placed it before Jim Welsh.

All the rustler-hunters crowded up to read. Win Evans said, 'Well now, Jim . . . ain't that a fright . . . why'd he use his real name?'

Barney answered that. 'Why not? This far an' after they been successful everywhere else—why not?'

Jim gazed at the station master with a finger on the paper. 'The feller who signed this—can you describe him?'

'Easy, mister, because of the two, Mister Moody an' that one, there wasn't no comparison. Mister Moody even smelled like a cattle buyer, but the other feller—Mister Knowlton—he was a town man if I ever saw one, skinny-brimmed hat down to his button shoes.'

Tad pulled the paper over, squinted and asked the station master a question. 'You know where this place is?'

The man with the eyeshade leaned, saw where Tad's finger was fixed, settled back and said, 'Sure I know. I was freight handler there for three years before gettin' promoted to my job down here.'

'Well, gawdammit, where is it?'

The station master was startled by Tad's

obvious irritation. 'It's north of Borderton about thirty miles. They ship a lot of livestock up there. It's good stock country with lots of big ranches.' The station master moved slightly from in front of Tad and addressed Jim Welsh. 'If they find out them cattle got the hoof-an-mouth disease in the slough grass country around that town—Fort Drum—they'll gang up'n shoot them cattle and ride them fellers who brought 'em out of town on a rail.'

Barney asked how large Fort Drum was and the station master answered readily. 'It's a cow town, pure an' simple. About half the size of Kingsville.'

Jim was straightening off the counter when he said, 'The feller at Fort Drum who sent the train down here for those cattle—what's his name?'

'Frank Bowdoin. He's from back East somewhere. He's been station master a long time.'

They went out on to the freight platform to palaver. Ben Hobart said, 'From what that man said, the distance's got to be about sixty more miles. That's two days of ridin'. By the time we get up there the cattle—will be sold an' Moody'n Knowlton will be gone.'

Barney went back into the station. When he returned ten minutes later he was downcast. 'No train's goin' north until maybe day after tomorrow when the next one's due from Clarendon.'

Jep had a suggestion. 'Take a stage from here. They change hitches, get fresh animals hooked on. Our animals been used pretty hard up to now.'

Without another word they trooped to the stage office where a young man entered the yard from a side door and stopped in his tracks. He had seen hard men before, but this was a whole crew of them.

Jim asked about the next coach going north from Kingsville. The stager answered without hesitation. 'It's bein' readied right now.' He paused, then said, 'It only holds four passengers—five with crowding.'

Pert Scovall said, 'How many on top?'

The stager considered the strangers again before answering. 'It'd be cold up there, gents.'

Barney snorted, then said, 'It go as far as Fort Drum?'

The younger man nodded. 'That's where the run ends, then it comes back to Kingsville.'

Jim handed money to the stager and led the way through a side door into the yard where a stage and six was being readied. The hostlers and whip paused to gaze at the party of faded, unsmiling strangers. The young stager said, 'All of 'em. Goin' up to Fort Drum.'

The whip, a thickset, lined man spat aside before speaking. 'The fellers on top'll likely freeze.'

Barney had an answer to that. 'You set up there.'

The whip pulled on his smoke-tanned gauntlets without another glance at Barney or the others, hitched at his britches, stepped from the nearside fore-wheel hub to a steel rung, got on to his seat, made sure his whip was in its socket, spat amber again and began evening up the lines.

Ben Hobart had one last question for the young stager. 'How long before we reach Fort Drum?'

'The coach'll make three stops, the last one at Borderton. It'll come into Fort Drum by mid-morning tomorrow.' He waited until the strangers were aboard then raised his hand to the whip, who talked up his horses, made a wide sashay past the log gates, got his hitch lined out and went north at a steady walk which he would hold to until the animals were warmed out.

Inside Jep said, 'First time I ever heard Barney say somethin' that made sense.'

The other men inside did not comment. The stage was one of those older ones with leather thoroughbrace springs. Later models had steel springs. The whip seemed to have a knack for hitting every rut. The fact that he handled the horses expertly meant they were more important to him than passengers.

Barney had insisted that Tad ride inside. Barney, Pert and Four Feathers rode on top, and it didn't wait for full night to be down before it got cold. They hunched up with their necks pulled down inside their coats like roosting sage hens. Not a word was said among them.

Inside, the conversation was perfunctory and Ben Hobart took no part in it. He slept; the hardest jolts did not awaken him.

Jep addressed Jim Welsh. 'If we don't find 'em up yonder . . .'

Jim nodded wearily and said nothing.

The whip chewed and expectorated over the side until Win poked out his head and said, 'Mister, you spray us one more time an' I'll climb up there an' cut your damned throat.'

It must have impressed the whip because he did not expectorate again until they reached the first way station. Then, as the hitch was being changed, he strolled over where the strangers were and said, 'Which one of you gents called me for spittin'?'

The whip was a solid, burly man who looked even more formidable in his heavy coat. While awaiting the answer he barely turned his head and spat amber; when he faced forward Win Evans was directly in front of him loosening the tie-down thong over his holstered Colt. Win said, 'I did an' if you always do that when you're drivin' it's a wonder to me someone hasn't cut your throat before now.'

The massive whip chewed, looked from one of them to the others, all of whom were watching him from closed faces, stopped chewing and turned slightly to expectorate again. Win Evans said, 'Do it, mister, an' you'll carry your guts home in a bucket.'

Win's right fingers were touching the saw-handle of his leathered six-gun.

The burly man stopped chewing, and slowly turned back to face Win.

Win said, 'Get your butt back up there . . . an' remember what I said: once more before we leave your coach an' I'll climb up there and cut your throat. *Get up there!*'

The whip went up the side of his coach, unlooped the lines and did not take his eyes off the rumps of the fresh hitch until Barney leaned and tapped him to indicate the passengers were aboard, then he kicked off the binders and talked up the horses.

It was cold enough to freeze the *cojones* off a brass monkey. Barney, who also chewed, rarely expectorated. Unlike the whip, Barney Miller was a lifelong tobacco chewer, the kind who did not expectorate once a cud was settled in his face.

He chewed now, rocking with the stage and wondering why Fate, or some busybody anyway, hadn't seen him born and raised somewhere other than west of the damned Missouri river.

They made the second stop at a way station which appeared as a wide clearing at the roadside completely surrounded with trees. The trees enhanced the darkness and did nothing to mitigate the cold.

The men from Cedarville clustered around the cannon heater inside while the horses were switched. They said nothing and the pair of hostlers who manned the station afterwards said if they hadn't been the Youngers or outlaws just as bad, it would be a consarned miracle.

They passed through Borderton without stopping. The place was as dark as the inside of a boot. They rattled out the north end with a light wind blowing, which added to their misery, more to the men on top than the men inside.

Barney leaned over next to the whip and said, 'Wasn't you supposed to change horses back there?'

The answer he got made it clear the whip wasn't going to stop again until he could get rid of this batch of passengers. Barney considered that, then said, 'Mister, you're lucky. That skinny feller you braced back yonder—his name is Cole Younger.'

The whip looked around, startled. Barney smilingly nodded his head. The whip sat forward, tended his horses and his lines and did not even loosen inside his thick coat until dawn arrived.

Amusement over the whip's reaction to the name Cole Younger kept Barney warm for the duration of the trip. Of course it was a lie but that didn't bother the old hand.

FORT DRUM AND BEYOND

When they left the corralyard at Ford Drum Pert said, 'You know what I think? That feller with the black sleeve garters back yonder was lied to pure an' simple. Them cattle they stole somewhere an' drove where that corral had been taken down didn't have no hoof-an' mouth disease. You can't drive cattle far that's sick with hoof-an' mouth.'

The others gazed at Pert without comment. Jim led off in search of a café.

Barney told Jep and Four Feathers what he'd told that cranky whip about Win being Cole Younger. Cold as they were, they laughed. The station master back at Kingsville was right, Fort Drum was a cow town stripped of all business which did not have to do with livestock. There was a way station, and north of it was a network of pole corrals that would hold close to five or six hundred cattle. Otherwise there was a mercantile, a saloon, a saddle and harness shop and a place where the proprietor made ends meet by doing gun repair and whiskey-making. The front of his shop where the gun work was done aromatically smelled of the back room where his pots and copper coils were. The gun works smelled stronger of working mash than did the saloon.

There was a café run by a Mexican woman no more than a couple of inches over five feet tall and who must have weighed close to three hundred pounds. She got around with astonishing agility for her size and when the men from Cedarville walked in she stopped dead still but showed nothing on her face. They sat down, told her they wanted breakfast and except for a demand for hot coffee left the rest of it up to her.

They were her first customers of the day, and for a fact she rarely had that many customers at one time any day of the year.

When she brought their food Jim asked who the town marshal was and got an answer he might have anticipated.

They did not have a lawman in Fort Drum. When something happened folks thought was bad, they ganged together and set it to rights.

He asked about the station master and the woman answered as impassively as she answered all questions. His name was Frank Bowdoin, he had been station master at Fort Drum so long he remembered when there was a log fort and soldiers during the Indian troubles.

She probably was curious about so many strangers arriving together but her expressionless face revealed nothing about that or, as they might learn, anything else.

101

The sun was climbing when they hunted down a dray master whose business was cartage but who also kept a couple of strings of saddle and harness animals he rented out. When they entered his yard the proprietor and a rawboned Indian woman were sitting in morning sunlight eating from bowls. They both stopped eating. The man, as whiskered as the pard with unkempt iron-grey hair, got to his feet. He was a good twenty years older than his woman, something which people in places like Fort Drum ignored. He held out a work-coarsened hand and said, 'Thaddeus Marcus. What can I do for you gents?'

Before Jim spoke the seated Indian woman arose, picked up both bowls and brushed close to Thaddeus Marcus as she said something which Marcus seemed not to have heard but which Four Feathers heard and understood.

Jim said they needed horses and outfits, something Thaddeus Marcus must have anticipated because his response was immediate. 'The animals I can let you have but I only got five saddles.' Thaddeus Marcus looked at Four Feathers. 'That 'un can ride bareback. They're used to it. How long'll you gents be needin' these horses?'

Jim shrugged. 'I can't say. Maybe a couple of days. Maybe more. We'll take care of 'em.'

Thaddeus Marcus was looking at stockmen. He did not doubt they would not abuse his animals. He was being sly when he said, 'I ain't

102

seen you boys around Drum. You cattle buyers by any chance?'

Jim shook his head but offered no other reply and Thaddeus Marcus blew out a long breath before speaking again. 'Gents, you got to understandI never saw none of you before in my life an' I got good sound animals which I paid good money for . . . you understand what I'm sayin'?'

Tad answered. 'We're not horse thieves, mister.' He jerked his head in Jim Welsh's direction. 'That gent owns the biggest outfit in the Cedarville country. I expect he could, if he was of a mind, buy you out of his watch pocket.'

Thaddeus Marcus was a fearless man, but he also went out of his way to avoid difficulties. He fixed his unblinking gaze on Tad. 'I don't like to put it this way, gents, but if you want horses an' outfits—you being strangers to me an' all—if someone amongst you will put up the price of the animals you can have 'em. Otherwise . . . you see my situation, gents?'

The tall Indian woman was standing in the doorway of a log house across the yard behind the men from Cedarville. Her right hand was behind her back.

Four Feathers nudged Jep and jerked his head. Jep saw the woman and faced forward with a soundless sigh. Thaddeus Marcus hooked both thumbs in his shellbelt. His expression was amiable but obdurate. After the silence had gone on as long as he thought it should he addressed Jim. 'You the head man?'

Jim nodded. 'Name's Welsh.'

'Mister Welsh put yourself in my boots. I worked years puttin' this business together. Look around. You see anythin' that'd make you believe folks in the Drum settlement are well off? I could make one bad judgement an' lose most of what I've spent fifteen years puttin' together.'

Jim said, 'How much money, Mister Marcus?'

'Well, you gents step over to the house. The missus'll make coffee. I never until this minute thought anythin' like this would happen. I got to figure on it. Come along.'

As Thaddeus Marcus led the way where the Indian woman was moving deeper into the house, Four Feathers moved to Jim's side and softly said, 'She told him we looked like horse thieves.'

Jim could believe that. None of them had shaved, their clothing was rumpled and stained. Anywhere they might have appeared folks would have reason to have a similar suspicion.

There were probably few people west of the Big River who carried around with them the kind of money Thaddeus Marcus required before handing over his animals and outfits.

The Indian woman brought them coffee. There were not enough chairs in the small parlour so she brought benches from a back room, then she stood in the kitchen doorway as silent and expressionless as one of those cigar-store Indians they had back East, except that she kept her right hand behind her back.

Jim shoved back his hat and leaned forward as he told Thaddeus Marcus the entire story beginning back in the Cedarville country when Will Devon had been raided.

It took time. The woman had to make a fresh pot of coffee. When Jim concluded with their arrival in Fort Drum without horses Thaddeus Marcus arose, mumbled something and went into the kitchen with his woman. The men in the parlour could hear every word they said but it made sense to only one of them, and Four Feathers who was of Siouian descent hadn't heard nor spoken his native language since late childhood. When there was a lull in the kitchen Four Feathers crossed to Jim's chair, leaned down and whispered, 'She told him if you don't have enough money to put up for the horses, he should either turn you down or go with us.'

Four Feathers went to the bench and sat down. Jim was ready when Thaddeus Marcus returned, offered coffee all around, got negative head wags and sat down considering Jim. 'Like I said, Mister Welsh, I just plain can't do it unless I got money in hand before you gents leave town.'

The Indian woman was back in the doorway with her hand behind her back. What Jim said to Thaddeus Marcus made her black eyes jump to Four Feathers and stay there. Jim said, 'Everything I told you was gospel truth. We're close to findin' the rustlers. They're somewhere in this territory. Mister Marcus, we come a long way, we can't finish it on foot an' we aren't goin' to turn back . . . you come with us. We'd like to have you along.'

Marcus did not look surprised, neither did his woman who continued to stare at Four Feathers, who deliberately avoided returning her understanding gaze.

Marcus arose; without a word or even a glance the woman reached behind a door where a gun and shellbelt were hanging, handed them to her man and went into another room to return with a booted saddlegun and a buckskin jerky pouch.

She spoke again in a language only Four Feathers knew a smattering of, but this time they didn't have to understand. Thaddeus Marcus was buckling the gun belt into place when he said, 'There's another reason I didn't want to let you have the animals, Mister Welsh.' He finished buckling the belt with a jerk and looked up. 'There's eight of 'em. One city feller, Mister Moody an' six riders.'

It was so quiet a pin falling would have sounded loud. Win Evans blew out a breath and put a sardonic glance on Jim Welsh before he said, 'You know that for a fact, do you, Mister Marcus?'

The barrel-built bewhiskered man nodded. 'They ain't exactly strangers. Last year they used our railroad corrals to load out quite a bunch of cattle. Among the local stockmen nothin' much was said. There was at least four different brands on them cattle, but like it was said, cattle buyers usually bought from more'n one outfit.'

Jep said, 'Can you describe 'em, Mister Marcus?'

'Not all of 'em although I saw 'em off an' on while they was around, but there was a stocky feller with whiskers who wore a city man's matchin' britches and coat, an' this time there was a feller with him, sort of skinny. He didn't look to me like a man who knew one end of a cow from the other.'

Jim said, 'Moody and Knowlton.' Several men nodded but Thaddeus Marcus didn't. He said, 'It's hard to believe. They been here before, paid good money at the store an' elsewhere, didn't make trouble. Mister Moody was real mannerly. Whatever was done for him he always said thank you.

Jep said, 'You knew him by name?'

'Everybody did. The last time they used our loading chute about a year ago they stayed around for about a week. That many strangers in a place no larger'n Fort Drum makes an impression. I'll tell you straight out I hope you're wrong, at least about Mister Moody.'

Jep had a question. 'How long ago did they ship out from here?'

'Three, four days ago.'

'Do you know anythin' about the train?'

'Only that it arrived a day or so after they corralled their cattle. The engineer's married to one of the Spencer girls, a daughter of Judd Spencer of JS ranch west of town.'

'What's his name, Mister Marcus?'

'Billy Hollister.'

Jim had been quietly thinking. Now he too asked a question. 'You got any idea where the train took those cattle?'

'Barely over the line, Mister Welsh, to a settlement of mostly homesteaders they call Freedom City. It's no city, it's mostly soddies, tent-shacks an'—'

'They unload at Freedom City?'

'Yes. Sell cattle to buyers from up-state an' the homesteaders.'

Barney spoke. 'How far is this Freedom City, Mister Marcus?'

'Not awful far. The state line's about three, four miles north. Freedom City's another three, four miles in a grassy swale with trees and a creek. Pretty place before them folks come and made it ugly with their settlement.'

Four Feathers addressed the expressionless woman leaning in the kitchen doorway, 'What time is it, ma'am?'

She looked back and answered him in her own language, and continued to regard him as he interpreted. 'Nigh on to eight o'clock. We could be up yonder in an hour or so.'

Thaddeus Marcus said, 'An' what if they're up there peddlin' cattle?'

Pert answered instantly. 'Hang every man jack of 'em.' Marcus looked long at Pert, then shrugged, winked at his woman and said, 'Let's get a-horseback, gents.'

The woman called to Marcus from her doorway. He did not answer but he waved as he continued walking. Barney sidled up to the 'breed. 'What did she say?'

'Somethin' about him being most of her heart so he had to come back.'

Barney made what was, for him, a surprising remark. 'She's a good woman, Feathers, an' they're mighty hard to find.'

Four Feathers looked around. 'A lot of 'em are, Barney.'

Barney spat aside, wiped his lips and looked straight ahead when he said, 'You'd never convince Mister Custer of that.'

Thaddeus Marcus hadn't lied about the quality of his animals. None of them would ever question him about that but Thaddeus Marcus wasn't a horse-rider—hell, anyone could ride a horse, all they had to do was spread their legs and pull a horse under them. Thaddeus Marcus was a horseman, meaning he knew more about horses on the ground

109

than most riders knew from the saddle.

While they were rigging out, one of the local tarpaper-shack men came to lean on the gate watching. By this time everyone who lived in Fort Drum and even somewhat beyond knew of the strangers. This sharp-nosed, lined and stringy man made a smoke, lighted it and strolled over where Marcus was handing out blankets, bridles and saddles. He said, 'What's goin' on, Thad? You know them boys?'

The bearded man spoke aside as he handed Four Feathers a bitting harness because he had already given away the saddles. 'I ain't sure, Hank, but I'm goin' along to watch out for my animals.'

The sharp-nosed man gazed casually around, stomped out his smoke and made his observation quietly. 'Look like a band of renegades to me. You know 'em?'

Marcus jutted his jaw in the direction of Jim. 'That one's named Welsh. Seems he's a big stockman over in the Cedarville country. Go talk to him, Hank, I got to get ready.'

In the haste of preparing to ride no one heeded the sharp-nosed man's departure. For that matter they hadn't paid any attention to him before he left. He was one of those nondescript individuals people see often without recollecting.

Information passed swiftly in a place like Fort Drum where few interesting or inexplicable things happened, so when they left town there were more discreet watchers from windows than there were outside, like the gunsmith and the saloonman, who waved out of habit.

Thaddeus Marcus rode in silence unless spoken to. He may have considered it his bounden duty to hunt down outlaws, most men did, but Jep's private opinion, formed after they had left the village behind, was that Marcus might be having second thoughts. He rode up beside the bearded man, said, 'This looks like good stock country.'

Marcus's reply was short. 'It is. Lots of grass, a fair amount of rain.'

The rangeboss tried again. 'Somethin' we never figured out; why Moody an' Knowlton used their real names.'

Marcus answered tersely, 'It wouldn't make a heap of difference, would it? They could be identified by descriptions.'

Jep nodded, said, 'I reckon,' and dropped back to ride with Tad and Barney. The older man had also studied Marcus. 'You expect he's beginnin' not to like what he's doin'? Sort of like betrayin' someone he knows?'

Jep shrugged and rode along in thoughtful silence. Pert, who was directly behind, said, 'Why didn't Jim tell him them cattle is supposed to have hoof-'n-mouth?'

Tad and Barney ignored Pert but Jep didn't. He answered irritably, 'Because they don't have it.'

Pert persisted. 'Hell, anybody'd know sick cattle if they seen them.'

This time the rangeboss, like the men he was riding with, looked straight ahead in silence.

Four Feathers turned in beside Thaddeus Marcus, said something the others did not understand, and Marcus looked at the 'breed when he answered in the same language. For some reason, perhaps because Marcus felt comfortable in his woman's language, he and Four Feathers rode together in conversation and once Four Feathers laughed. Marcus smiled, spoke again and Four Feathers forgot and replied in English. 'That's the truth. Biggest mistake they made was to let their women take up with whites.'

Marcus replied in English. 'How about you—you taken up with 'em?'

Four Feathers made Barney smile. He said, 'I was raised white. I'm only In'ian on the outside.'

They halted where a mound of whitewashed large stones had been neatly piled to form a sort of pyramid. Marcus said, 'Not much farther. This is the boundary between Colorado an' Wyoming.'

The country changed; it was less rugged, had fewer fields of rocks, more grass and even some timber, but for that there were a hundred stumps for every standing tree. Something like this indicated a settlement was close but they saw no sign of it until they encountered two faded, unshorn, hard-looking men driving a wagon.

They yielded the right of way. The men stopped to talk but the men from Cedarville only nodded as they passed.

The wagoners turned on the seat to watch them. One of them spoke to the other one. 'That was Thad Marcus.' The other man nodded. 'What'n hell's he doin' ridin' with a band that looked to me like renegades?'

The first man straightened around, flipped the lines and said, 'We'll likely find out when we get back. I wish someone'd set up a mill at the settlement. Folks waste time goin' down to Fort Drum every time they run out of flour an' salt.'

His companion's reply was blunt. 'It's like peein' in a creek to raise the tide to tell folks to smoke and bottle the damned meat, then they wouldn't need so much other stuff.'

The country improved, almost as though the dividing line between Colorado and Wyoming had been made according to this change.

Marcus left the road, led the men behind him westerly. In the distance they saw smoke rising from a scattering of shacks and soddies. Some of those homesteader buildings were much farther out but none were farther than the sound of a gunshot.

Jim and Jep were riding together through grass that brushed their stirrups. Jep said,

113

'Why'n hell did the cowmen let squatters get started here? This is as good a stock country as we got at home.'

Jim agreed, in part anyway. He had grown up before squatters were a threat. He had recognized the inevitable, so there were squatters on the edge of his range, but not very many. Like everyone else homesteaders had to have water, and Long Bow had deed to most of the watered acreage for miles.

Two men and a woman drying her hands on an apron came out to watch the riders pass. Jim waved, the squatters waved back and continued to watch the riders for a long time.

Barney made a dry remark. 'Good thing them folks don't have a telegraph between their houses.' Tad and Four Feathers looked blankly at Barney. That was the kind of remark they would have expected from Pert but not from the top hand.

Marcus rode a long ways westward and only stopped where creek willow as thick as hair on a dog's back backgrounded them.

He dismounted, held a rein in his left hand and pointed with the other. 'See that timbered knoll north-easterly from the settlement?' He dropped his arm. 'On the far side is a set of pole corrals. See them wagon tracks goin' around the base of the hill? Pretty worn ain't they? Well, them marks was made by settlement folks goin' behind the hill to barter for cattle.' Marcus closed both hands over the

114

horn of his saddle. Because it was always next to impossible to read the expression of a bearded man, the others could only judge what Marcus had said by his voice. It had sounded inflectionless and matter-of-fact.

Barney exchanged a look with Tad. They were thinking the same thing. Now that they were likely to have a showdown, Marcus was not at all happy.

The sun was high and the day was warm without being hot; visibility was good—too good for a party of armed riders to move toward that knoll.

They were a mile or such a matter west of the knoll. While they sat considering what to do, a solitary rider loped on an easterly angle toward the worn wagon road which led around behind the hill and followed around the base of it until they could no longer see him.

Pert said, 'Maybe that's one of 'em.'

The others ignored that, they were concerned with how to get around the hill, get behind it, without being detected. Pert made another remark and this time while no one spoke, what he had said was a possibility none of them like to think about.

'Suppose Mister Moody an' the Clarendon banker ain't over there?'

8

WAITING

Four Feathers offered to scout. Jim considered the offer and eventually nodded as he said, 'Be damned careful.'

Four Feathers left them riding at a walk and angling northward. They saw him fade from sight well above Freedom City then removed their outfits and hobbled the animals so they could graze, and sat down to get comfortable in tree shade. It could be a long wait.

Marcus stoked up a pipe in silence, lit up and got comfortable with his back to a creek willow. He considered the north-easterly territory as solemn as an owl. Eventually he addressed Jim Welsh. 'They peddle cattle over yonder. I don't know for a fact but I've been told buyers come down from up north an' drive away sizeable bands.' He puffed up a head of smoke before removing the pipe to also say, 'They ain't popular with the squatters because they got to have cash on the barrel head or its equivalent. Sometimes, so I been told, that means tradin' their work horses, whatever jewelry their womenfolk still got, their guns.'

Pert spoke up. 'Their guns? How do they hunt—bows an' arrers?'

Marcus had to relight the pipe so he took his time replying. It wasn't possible to carry on much of a conversation without a pipe going out. 'The ones that still got guns do the huntin'. That's what I've heard. Personally I don't know many of those folks an' don't come up here unless I can't squirm out of it. Haul in supplies now'n then . . . I guess it's a starve-out proposition. Every spring a few wagons go through Drum with worn-out-lookin' women and kids that don't smile.'

Pert had another question. 'Why'n hell they come out here in the first place?'

This time before answering Thaddeus Marcus removed the pipe, knocked it clear of dottle and pocketed it. 'Free land. I expect that sounds real temptin' to folks with nothin', living in crowded, dirty cities back East. The trouble is, if they don't take a close look and go somewhere else, if they settle in a place like Freedom City, directly they run out of money, then they can't move.'

Pert picked up a twig and drew designs in the dirt at his feet, scowling.

They watched people moving in the squalid little settlement. Women draped grey wash from ropes stretched between buildings or trees, children played in the dirt, men cut wood from trees which had been dragged a considerable distance. Marcus said bitterly, 'That's the only thing that's free. Every winter kids die, the wood gives out. Gents, folks who take up land in this country without money to live on until they can get set up, is fools pure an' simple.'

Barney asked Marcus how long he'd been in the country and got a forthright answer. 'I never kept track of time. I was here before the cow outfits settled in, before the soldiers come and made wood stockades. I lived with my woman's people six years, trappin', huntin', stealin' horses with the In'ians. They didn't steal cattle unless they had to. They like horse meat better'n cow meat.' Marcus shifted and got resettled. 'There's some big cow outfits hereabouts. If those rustlers been stealin' off them it might take a little time but the stockmen'll find out an' when they do—'

Ben Hobart interrupted. 'Moody'n his bunch might be long gone. They danged near put me out of the cow business. It ain't like I had many cattle like them big outfits. Mister Marcus, I don't particularly want to shoot them sons of bitches, I want to set astraddle of 'em one at a time an' choke the bastards to death no matter how long it'll take to catch 'em.'

A youngster astraddle a gaunt jenny mule, bare-back and with twine reins on a bridle with blinders was coming toward them.

He seemed hesitant, which was understandable. That many rumpled, unshaven, heavily armed men sitting in willow shade with horses grazing behind them would make warning bells ring in the back of most minds.

He was barefoot, had skinny arms, pants frayed up past the ankles which were held up by a piece of twine reaching from in front on the left side, up across and made fast behind on the right side.

He was freckled and hadn't been sheared in a long time. He rode up, stopped, leaned on the mule's neck soberly looking at the men sitting in the shade. He said, 'My name's Ulysses Bannion. My paw was a Union soldier in the war. He got shot in the hip an' don't track real good. Who are you gents?'

Barney answered, 'Just fellers passin' through. Do they call you Ulysses?'

'No sir, my maw'n paw call me Ned. Was you in the war, mister?'

Barney smiled. 'Best to let sleepin' dogs lie, Ned. That was long ago. Best to forget it.'

'My paw don't forget it. He can tell stories that'll keep you awake half the night.'

Marshal Evans ended this topic by asking a question. 'You folks got plenty of beef, have you?'

Ned faced Win Evans by shifting his leaning position which did not bother the mule. Most likely not many things bothered the mule. It had sunken places over each eye where the hair was grey. Mules lived a long time, usually much longer than horses. During that long time they got to know two-legged things better'n most two-legged things knew themselves.

The mule stood hipshot with both eyes closed as Ned answered the rangeboss's question. 'My maw put up a lot of meat. I heard 'em talkin' when they figured I was asleep in the trundle bed. She told Paw she wasn't sure we could last out another winter.'

Marshal Evans got the topic back to beef. 'Your folks buy beef from them gents got the corrals behind that knoll, do they?'

Ned answered without hesitation. 'Well, up until lately. Paw run out of money.'

Jim had a question for the lad. 'Those gents behind that hill—do you know them?'

'No sir, not me, but my paw does.'

'How many are back there, Ned?'

'They usually drive in cattle; Paw says maybe five or six riders and couple of other gents are waitin' at the corrals. I don't know ciphers; how many would that be?'

'Eight,' Jim said.

'Is that as many as you gents?'

Jim smiled. 'Close, Ned.'

Barney got to his feet, dusted his britches and dug into a pocket as he approached the youngster. The others watched as Barney told the boy to hold out his hand. When he did the top hand put money into it and closed the lad's fingers. 'Tell your maw I once had a lad an' for her to take you down to the mercantile in Fort Drum an' get you fitted out with some decent clothes.'

Ned partially opened his fingers, peeked in, clenched his fist, stared with wide eyes at Barney and said, 'Mister, I'm more obliged than I know how to—'

Barney took the mule by the bridle, smiled up at the lad and patted the mule on the rump. He stood with his back to the others until he could no longer see the lad among the shanties, then turned, avoided the eyes of his companions, sat down and let go a rattling breath before saying, 'I had a lad about like him once.'

No one spoke. Pert almost did but Jep jammed him hard in the ribs and scowled.

Better than an hour later Tad raised an arm. The rider was coming from the north at an easy lope. He wasn't riding toward the settlement, he was far too far west for that but they could not identify him for some time, then it was Tad who said, 'Feathers.'

The sun was well off-centre when the 'breed drew rein and while off-saddling and hobbling the horse he said, 'They got two corrals. Both is full of cattle. They're bawlin' their heads off. They ain't been fed or watered. It was too far to make out brands.'

Pert took the horse out to graze and Four Feathers sat on the sweaty saddleblanket as he told them the rest of it. 'There's ten men over there.' He paused to look at Thaddeus Marcus. 'An' your friend from the corralyard down at Fort Drum.' At the blank look that remark made, Four Feathers said, 'The scrawny feller who leaned on the gate then went back an' talked to you.'

There was a moment of chilly silence as Hobart, Evans and the Long Bow men looked steadily at Thaddeus Marcus. What they were thinking Pert put into words. 'You double-crossed us, did you, Mister Marcus?'

The bearded man spoke loudly. 'Hank. That son of a bitch. He asked what we was about. I told him to go ask Mister Welsh. I never told him a damned thing. If he's over there he must have follered us, then struck out on his own. That's the gospel truth.'

The silence ran on. Ben Hobart dug out his wicked-bladed clasp knife, picked up a twig and went to whittling. He did not raise his eyes until Jim said, 'There won't be any surprise. Not now, an' I was counting on that.'

Hobart held his knife aloft in one hand, the little stick in the other hand as he looked at Thaddeus Marcus. 'You didn't tell that son of a bitch what we was about?'

Marcus was sweating and breathing hard. 'I swear it on the Bible. When he asked what we was about I told him to go ask Mister Welsh. I was too busy to talk.'

Pert spoke. 'He left off back there where you'n him was talkin', walked right past me an' out the front gate. He never went near Jim.'

Ben snapped his knife closed and stood up

looking in the direction of the knoll. Whether he was satisfied with Marcus's story or not, when he spoke it was a different topic. 'How many did you say, Feathers?'

'Six riders, the bearded feller wearin' a suit, a skinny feller without no hat, and two other men. I got no idea who they are.'

Hobart still gazed in the direction of the knoll when he spoke again. 'That makes ten of 'em.'

Win Evans nodded his head. 'Even if that feller Mister Marcus talked to is over there, has told 'em we're on their trail, we can still make out.' Win looked at Four Feathers. 'Can you get us around behind 'em after dark?'

The 'breed's dark eyes flashed. 'That's no question to ask a man.'

'Well . . . what we need to do first off is sneak around over there after dark an' set them sons of bitches on foot. After that we got to figure out what to do next.' Evans again looked at the 'breed. This time Four Feathers did not wait for the question. He swallowed his jerky, wiped grease off his hands on his britches and said, 'If that son of a bitch from Fort Drum told 'em about us they'll sure as hell be watchin' like hawks.'

Evans replied dryly, 'I know all that . . . can you sneak us around over there?'

Four Feathers answered with confidence. 'Yes, but you got to leave your spurs behind where we tie the horses. There's trees atop that knoll, but there's more trees northward an' westerly.'

Marshal Evans looked at Jim Welsh, who had thus far taken no part in the conversation. He nodded at Win Evans. 'Carbines, six-guns an' no spurs where we leave the horses.'

Barney said, 'When?'

Jim looked at the sky. The sun was still up there but was getting dust-reddened as it sank. 'Couple of hours,' Welsh said.

It had to be agreeable to all of them but Barney got up and moved around. His behind was numb from so much sitting. He and Tad went out where the animals were cropping feed. Tad asked if Barney believed what Thaddeus Marcus had said, and Barney's reply did not answer the question. 'We come this far, got shrunk to nubbins, ain't had a decent night's sleep since we left Long Bow, so it don't matter what I believe, boy. What matters is whether we can sneak around and catch them bastards even if they know we're comin'.'

Tad was frankly uneasy. 'I wish I'd known that son of a bitch was friendly with them cow thieves. I'd have shot him in the corral.'

Barney said nothing. He stood watching the sun go infinitesimally lower.

Jep came out to join them and stood in silence until Barney faced around, then all the rangeboss did was raise his eyebrows. Barney flickered a little smile. 'You notice Win don't go around Ben Hobart very much?'

Jep hadn't watched them. He said, 'I'm havin' trouble over Mister Marcus.'

Tad spoke. 'Me too, if you want to know. Only, why would he ride with us if he sent that feller to warn the cow thieves?'

Jep's reply was short. 'That's what's botherin' me.'

Barney did not join in this discussion. He turned back to watching as the red sun teetered on some distant hazed upthrusts. Jep nudged Tad. They started back. When they were some distance back Jep said, 'That kid he gave money to . . .'

'What about him?'

'Did you know Barney had a wife an' a son who got drowned in a flashflood?'

Tad's eyes widened. 'Him'n me been ropin' together since I got hired on an' he never told me that.'

Jep was not surprised. Barney had only told him when he had been falling-down drunk in Cedarville years back, and Jep doubted that Barney would even remember telling him. Also, this was the first time Jep had ever told a soul.

'Somethin' else,' Jep said. 'You ever notice how he hovers over you, takes your side in arguments, worried about how you could stand it when we had to ride out?'

This time the younger man hiked along scowling at the ground before speaking. 'Yeah. But I figured that's because we are a team at the marking ground.'

Jep softly said, 'It could be. For a fact it could be.' He did not say another word all the way back to the place where their riding equipment had been indifferently piled and where Jim and the lawman were sitting in failing light talking desultorily.

Barney did not come back from where the horses were cropping feed for another hour. By that time dusk was creeping in and Jim thought it was about time to ride.

He did not want to wait until full dark because Four Feathers might have trouble taking them where Jim wanted them to be.

He could have saved himself that anxiety, Four Feathers could have led them in pitch dark.

10

A NIGHT TO REMEMBER

There was smoke rising among the shanties of Freedom City. Because there was no breeze it hung in the air, and while smoke from supper fires normally was a pleasant scent, not this time. The light was barely good enough to see the condition of the shanties from which the smoke was rising.

Pert said, 'No dogs. You fellers notice—they

got no dogs. I never seen a settlement that didn't have dogs.'

No one commented until they were far enough on their way that only a few lights showed, then Barney said, 'Most likely ate their dogs.'

Pert didn't like that. 'What'n hell you talkin' about? Folks don't eat dogs!'

Barney was looking at the back of Four Feathers when he replied, 'Yes they do. Sioux eat dogs. Their favourite is white dog.'

Four Feathers neither looked around nor spoke, but the squaw man among them did. 'When you got nothin' to eat with maybe three foot of snow on the ground, you eat anythin' you can lay your hands on.'

No one kept this discussion going, least of all Four Feathers or the squaw man from Fort Drum.

They eventually lost sight of the lights back yonder. Four Feathers led them across a badly rutted north-south wagon road as well as across the railroad tracks which paralleled the wagon road with a fair distance between.

Four Feathers angled north-easterly where even in semi-darkness it was possible to skyline trees, tier after tier of them, mostly on high ground. The ones unfortunate enough to have grown on flat ground had been cut down and hauled to Freedom City long ago.

When they got into the uplands where it was totally dark, they thread-needled among the trees for a fair distance before Four Feathers stopped again. This time he did not have to say a word.

They were now north-east of the knoll and there were three small fires visible. Jim rode up beside the 'breed to ask how far he had scouted on ahead.

Four Feathers replied while watching those supper fires, 'Maybe half a mile. Why?'

'We got to get down and come in behind them,' Welsh replied.

Without another word the 'breed led off continuing to see-saw among the trees, some of which were huge and very tall. If the squatters figured how to get up here, cut logs and get them down to flat country, the trees wouldn't last long.

Thaddeus Marcus rode in front of Ben Hobart, and for a fact Ben would always be behind him. If Marcus noticed he seemed not to care.

They arrived in a small lightning-strike clearing of no more than ten acres. Four Feathers swung off and began tugging the latigo loose. Barney rode up beside him. 'That's goin' to be at least a mile back, Feathers.'

The 'breed grinned as he grunted the saddle off and dumped it in the grass, then knelt to remove the hobbles from aft of the cantle. He did not say a word.

Jim walked up leading his mount. Barney

128

turned away in disgust. In Barney's opinion of all the bad things that could happen to a man none were worse than being afoot, having to stumble around in the dark for a mile in a damned forest.

He watched Tad arrive in the little clearing, dismount and fling up his left-side stirrup leather. Barney shook his head and did the same.

They hobbled the animals in grass to their knees, came together with Winchesters in hand and waited for the 'breed to lead off. Jim Welsh had a question for Hobart, who had made the tabulation back near the creek willows. 'Ten, you said?'

Ben repeated it. 'Ten.'

'That feller from Fort Drum should have been there. That'd make eleven.'

Hobart considered Jim Welsh briefly before replying, 'The figure I come up with was ten men. That's how many the In'ian come up with.'

Win Evans got into the discussion by suggesting a reason for the discrepancy. 'Maybe the feller from Drum went back after warnin' the rustlers.'

No one agreed nor disagreed. Jim made a gesture for the 'breed to lead off, and Four Feathers did.

As soon as the sun set the cold arrived. The rustler-hunters were less concerned with that than they were in groping their way ahead because there was no moon. Even if it eventually arrived the chance of moonlight coming through all those tree tops was unlikely.

Four Feathers set his course according to the supper fires which at that distance were little more than pinpricks of brightness.

He took his time. Once he went nearer the edge of the hill, stood a while before returning to strike out again. He gave no reason for what he had done and no one asked. They made very little noise; a century and more of carpeting pine and fir needles muffled sound.

The last time the 'breed stopped the little fires showed more clearly. He turned toward Jim. 'Their animals got to be pretty much even to where we are now. It's big open place.'

Jim nodded and gestured toward the southerly side-hill. Before starting down Four Feathers spoke again. 'There's no cover once we get down there.'

Win Evans sounded irritable when he said, 'They can't see in the dark no better'n we can.'

Four Feathers picked his way carefully. As soon as they left the trees their footsteps were no longer soundless. Barney stepped on a flat piece of grey flint and had to jump to catch his balance. He swore under his breath and Tad grinned which Barney did not see.

When they reached flat land they had an unsettling experience. Two hobbled horses loomed out of the darkness. One threw up his head and snorted. He would have fled except for the hobbles. Barney swore again. This time Tad did not smile. On a dark, utterly still night that snort could be heard a considerable distance.

Four Feathers shortened his stride and halted often in order to find other horses and to avoid them. Ben Hobart came up beside Jim. 'I thought we was goin' to set 'em afoot,' he said quietly and Jim nodded, went ahead to reach the 'breed and mention their purpose in being over here. Four Feathers listened, nodded and said, 'Most of 'em are ahead. We set two or three loose'n they stampede, maybe right down past them fires.'

They continued with the small fires clear and the sound of an occasional voice audible before the 'breed paused to gesture with an upraised arm.

In the middle distance a number of horses were motionless, ears cocked in the direction of the intruders. They changed course and made no haste. The horses were less frightened than they were curious. Tad and Barney chummed in among them with soothing words. It did not always work but it did this time.

They went to work removing hobbles, some of which were Mormon loop-throughs and others were army surplus chain hobbles. The horses stood still. When they had freed six head the men eased back as quietly and slowly as they had approached. The horses watched them go, dropped their heads and resumed grazing. Pert shook his head, most of the horses he'd freed from hobbles busted out in a run. But he did not mention this, mainly because no one talked now and everyone was doing his best to move as stealthily as possible without making a sound.

Four Feathers raised an arm, halted, twisted and beckoned to Ben Hobart. The others knelt to minimize being skylined and watched the 'breed and the stump rancher move like ghosts slightly northward.

Nearby the freed horses grazed along in the easterly direction of the horses which had not been freed. They had to have the scent of men in their nostrils but except for giving them a wide berth they did not heed them at all.

Tad leaned toward Barney. 'Where'd they go?'

Barney said, 'Shut up.'

The silence was broken twice, once by a man swearing, the other time by someone laughing. Win leaned close to Jim. 'Better laugh while they can.

For some reason, probably because of hoarseness from bawling all day, the corralled cattle were quiet.

Four Feathers and Ben Hobart returned half dragging a man between them. They let him fall in front of Jim and the lawman. Whatever had happened to him had kept on happening. He had a smashed mouth, a gashed cheek, his filthy shirt was soaked, and although it was not immediately noticeable in the night, he had one puffy eye which was closing fast.

Ben said, 'Son of a bitch went out to pee. Feathers heard him.' Hobart lightly kicked the kneeling man. 'Talk you bastard. I'd as leave cut your throat as look at you. *Talk!*'

The man was not young but neither was he old. He had two close-spaced small eyes astraddle of a long, pointy nose. He was filthy. Even in the dark he smelled rank. He raised a hand to his battered face and looked steadily at Jim Welsh who asked his name. The answer was slurred. 'Larry Herman.' The man settled closer on the ground. He was hurt and in pain, there was no doubt of that. Jim looked at Four Feathers, who jerked his head in Ben Hobart's direction. 'Jumped him from behind before I could get up.'

Hobart was regarding the prisoner showing no expression except up around the eyes and it was too dark for that to show.

Jim asked the man how many men were around the corrals and again there was no hesitation. 'Ten countin' me.'

Jim asked where the man was who had come from Fort Drum to warn the man's friends they were being followed. Again the answer came swiftly. 'Hank? Mister Moody give him two cartwheels an' he rode easterly.'

Barney said, 'Mister Moody's down there?'
'Yes.'

'An' Mister Knowlton?'

'No. He left. Said he had to get back to Clarendon.' The rustler spat blood and groped for a filthy bandanna to hold to his mouth. He was recovering from the beating but was clearly frightened. He looked at the men carrying carbines, all but Ben Hobart, he would not look at him.

Hobart sank to one knee beside the rustler, leaned on his carbine and spoke in a quiet, inflectionless voice. 'If that feller from down yonder told Moody we was lookin' for him, how come Moody didn't high-tail it?'

'Two buyers come along. They're with Mister Moody. He had to wait. They bought the cattle an' hired four of us to drive 'em north come daylight.'

'Did Moody tell the buyers they bought rustled cattle?' For the first time the outlaw looked at Hobart. 'Course not,' he said, and faced Jim again.

Pert asked a question. 'Where'd them cattle come from, this time?'

'Thirty miles south-west, from an outfit that brands with a mule shoe with the letter G inside.'

Win Evans was bothered by the lack of anxiety among the rustlers after they had been warned they were being hunted. He asked the rustler why any of them were still there, knowing they were being hunted.

Larry Herman had to wipe off blood. It was becoming increasingly difficult to understand him. His torn mouth was swelling by the minute.

'The feller from Drum said he didn't pass you on the way, so he figured you went off westerly somewhere.'

Barney let go a long breath and wagged his head. For the time being the others were content to gaze at the beaten outlaw and say nothing, but eventually Four Feathers said the outlaw's friends would be wondering what was taking him so long, and that brought all eyes back to the man with the filthy, bloody shirt. Ben Hobart shoved back upright, leaned and produced a boot knife with a double-edged blade.

The outlaw cringed and Jep said, 'Put up the knife.' They stood looking at one another until Jim Welsh said the same thing. Hobart hoisted his lower trouser leg, sheathed the knife without saying a word.

Pert asked how far to the first supper fire. The outlaw was still cringing when he answered, 'About a hunnert feet from where they jumped me.'

Jim considered the outlaw; he was close to collapsing from fear and pain. 'Barney, lash him real good.'

Tad helped. First they used the man's belt to bind his ankles then they took the bloody bandanna and lashed his arms at the wrists behind his back. Pert asked what had happened to the man's sidearm and Ben answered, 'I flung it as far as I could.' Ben then produced a nickel-plated under-and-over .41 calibre bellygun with a three-inch barrel. He broke it open, pocketed two loads, snapped it closed and dropped it on the outlaw.

Four Feathers led off again, this time in the direction of the nearest fire. The rangeboss got close to his employer and whispered, 'Win's right, Hobart'll kill real easy.'

Jim did not speak but he nodded his head and looked around where Ben Hobart was again walking behind Thaddeus Marcus, who had not said a word back yonder.

They unexpectedly came upon a hobbled saddle mule. The long-eared animal was as surprised as the men were. It looked at them down its long face, ears forward, seemingly waiting to see what came next.

Win walked forward talking quietly. Unlike a horse in a similar situation, the mule remained relaxed and watchful. He did not fidget or offer to shy. When Win kept talking soothingly as he ran a hand along the mule's neck to the shoulder then down the animal's leg the mule stood like a rock. Win unbuckled the hobbles, left them in the grass and slowly arose, still talking.

He gave the mule a gentle pat and started back to join the others. The mule had found a friend; he followed Win. Barney was grinning when the marshal came up and turned. The mule was less than four feet behind him. Barney very quietly said, 'Mister Evans, if you'd been around mules much you wouldn't have given him that last pat. It's a mule's nature to need a friend. I've seen 'em take up with a chicken, a kid or a dog, foller 'em everywhere but in the house.'

Marshal Evans faced the mule. Ben Hobart said, 'Hit him. Drive him off.'

Instead Win Evans spoke to the mule and stroked its long face. Barney audibly sighed, turned to Jim and spoke quietly, 'It's goin' with us. Can't do no harm. Let's go.'

True enough as the men started toward the nearest fire the mule singled out Marshal Evans and plodded along directly behind Jim. Under different circumstances there would have been smiles. Now, no one smiled.

When they were within shouting distance of the nearest fire the mule brayed, a sound once heard was never forgotten. It was the braying of a jackass but with the bugle-like loudness of a horse.

They stopped stone-still and dropped low in the grass as a man called out, 'Mister, what's-your—name, your mule is in our camp.'

There was no answer, but the sound of a large man coming in the direction of the mule was audible every step of the way.

The rustler-hunters fanned out and became

invisible against the ground as a large, pot-bellied man wearing a large grey hat materialized, went up to the mule—as close as fifteen feet from the hunkering lawman—reached for the mane as he said, 'Damn animal, I'll find a horse for you to partner with.' The mule dug in his heels. The large man pulled harder. The mule sat back. The large man lost patience. 'Stubborn son of a bitch,' he said, released the mane and stepped away to kick the mule in the side. He did not get his boot off the ground. Something hit him from behind with considerable force. The man squawked, went down in the grass and Marshal Evans hit him over the head with his carbine barrel.

For ten seconds there was not a sound then a voice was raised near the little fire. 'Hey, mister cattle buyer, you all right? Did the mule kick you?'

Jim gestured frantically. His companions arose like wraiths hurrying in the direction of the fire. Thaddeus Marcus was in the forefront. The cattle thieves around the fire saw him first and came up to their feet. One of them started to say something when men came out of the darkness on all sides of them and Ben Hobart cocked his handgun.

The rustlers were silent except for a man who coughed, but that did not last long.

The silence was broken only by the crackling sounds of the little fire. Jim's companions went up close, flung weapons away and pushed the rustlers back to the ground. There were four of them. Barney whispered to Tad, 'That whittles down the odds,' then went over where a nondescript-looking man was glaring at Thaddeus Marcus. Barney put his cold handgun barrel into the man's ear and said, 'Where's Moody?' When the man glaring at Marcus did not reply Barney hit him on the head with his pistol barrel and moved toward the next man, who was dark, darker than Four Feathers and who, when he spoke, had an accent none of them could immediately identify. He was a Mexican, dark, squatty, venomous-looking, but evidently wise enough to speak before Barney got behind him. He raised a hand and pointed toward a more distant fire. 'Over there,' he said, and lowered his arm, twisted and looked up at Barney.

Neither of them said another word. The fire the Mexican had pointed to was closer to the corral. Jim Welsh told Pert to stay with the disarmed men and led the others in the direction of that distant fire.

Altogether there were three little fires. One had been neutralized. The farthest fire was past a nearer one to the south. They bypassed that one by going north-west for a considerable distance and returning on the far side of the corral where the smell of cattle was strong.

Jim gestured for men to go around from the south while he and Evans and Marcus would slip around from the north. Ben Hobart, who would be separated from Marcus with this diversion, deliberately disobeyed and remained with Jim and the lawman so he could continue to shadow Thaddeus Marcus.

They were too close to three men around the fire on the east side of the corral to speak back and forth, so as the men split up, although Win and Jim were annoyed with Hobart they said nothing.

The cattle were aroused by strong man-scent on both sides of the corral. Several heaved up to their feet. This encouraged other cattle to do the same. They began their bawling, kept it up until all the corralled animals joined in a chorus that would reach as far as Freedom City and beyond.

The men at the nearest fire continued to pass a bottle around and the men at the more distant fire reacted to the aroused cattle in a way that indicated they were seasoned outlaws and indifferent to the thirst and hunger of the cattle. They were more interested in feeding twigs into their fires to keep warm.

Jim had no time to speculate about what was going to happen. He, Win, Marcus and Hobart were slipping along the south side of the corral where they could clearly make out three men who were backgrounded by a little fire.

Finally, these individuals were aroused, straightened up to look in the direction of the corrals.

Jim held out his arm. He and his companions froze. It was doubtful that the men at the fire could make them out but the arrival of another man out of the easterly night changed everything.

It was impossible to hear what the newcomer was saying but it was easy to guess. The sitting men came up to their feet. The man who had come from the fire was on the far side where firelight limned him very well. He was a stranger to Win and Jim but not to Thaddeus Marcus who whispered to Jim. 'That's Toughy Bartle. I knew him from hangin' around Fort Drum waitin' for Moody to arrive.'

Of the other pair, one was lean and clearly a rangeman while the other was slightly portly wearing britches and pants that matched. This man easily, clearly from long habit, moved his right hand to sweep his coat back and expose an ivory-handled six-gun.

From somewhere southward and westerly a single gunshot blew the dark silence apart. A splinter of corral stringer peeled off close to Ben Hobart whose reaction was both instinctive and very fast. He fired back. Evidently he had missed as his invisible challenger had also missed, but those two gunshots spoiled the stalk. Guns showed red muzzle-blasts from several different directions and the cattle repeatedly hit the pole gate until it broke. They they poured out of the corral bawling and blindly running.

It was pure pandemonium, dust rose, cattle trampled blankets, saddlery, even the little fires. Men squawked in an effort to escape being run over. Several fired their weapons into the air, but these cattle, half crazed with thirst and hunger, were blindly charging. Gunshots under ordinary conditions would have turned them but not this time.

11

MULESHOE G

The sound of cattle and gunshots completely drowned out another sound, resonating louder from the direction of Freedom City. No one distinguished this new sound from the other sounds nor were the men likely to make that distinction when they were fighting in a pandemonium that made them concentrate on two imminent perils, being run over by cattle or shot at from several different directions on a night so dark it was impossible to be sure of targets.

The men with Jim Welsh heard men yelling in a north-easterly direction. Ben Hobart, as calm as a man could be, snapped off a shot in the direction of the men by the nearest fire, which scattered them like quail, then spoke to Jim. 'They can't find their horses.'

Jim heard without heeding. He was watching a lump on the ground barely visible by reflected firelight. The lump started crawling. Jim fired in front of it. A stout man sprang up, fired at Jim's muzzle blast then ran like a deer. He sashayed as he did this so Jim's next shot missed him.

The darkness, enhanced by clouds of dust raised by the crazed cattle produced an atmosphere of total confusion. Men yelled, but there was no way of knowing which men did that. An abrupt fusillade of gunshots erupted easterly. Men yelled and as abruptly as this exchange occurred it ended. Two men were trying to reach the north side of the corrals. Jim, Tad, Marcus and Ben Hobart were facing eastward when the marshal's long-eared friend brayed, startling Jim and his companions who swung to see what had upset the mule. Jim's first thought was that the animal had been hit by a bullet, but the mule was on the far side of the corral where Win and his companions were barely visible from the south side of the corral. Someone over there cursed and fired a pistol at the same time. Whoever he was he had made a bad mistake. The return fire was fast and thunderous. Evidently there had been two of them because with echoes still audible the men on the south side of the corral could hear someone running. Jim called northward. 'Win? You fellers all right?'

The answer came belatedly. 'Feathers got hit.'

That resonant sound which had been barely distinguishable from the direction of Freedom City was now loud enough for the battlers behind the knoll to hear it during occasional lulls in their fight. Jim paused to listen as Marcus said, 'Horsemen!'

Jim shucked casings from his six-gun and was plugging in fresh loads when Ben Hobart added to what Marcus had said. 'If they're friends of them rustlers we're in hot water up to our gills.'

Jim finished reloading and listened, but several gunshots eastward made him swear. When that noise ended he could clearly hear riders. They were coming in a lope. It sounded like a fair-sized number of them. He had to make a fast decision. He called to the men on the north side of the corral. They started around to join Jim and the others.

Everyone could hear those riders now but it was too dark to make them out. Everyone but Jim Welsh got busy punching out spent casings and reloading.

The approaching riders eventually became as audible as the stampeding cattle had been earlier. No one said anything until Pert spoke. 'Sounds like the damned army.'

144

Thad Marcus said, 'I hope it is.'

It wasn't.

A man who had lost his hat came out of the darkness sounding like a bellows as he ran. He saw the crowd beside the corral at the same time they saw him. He stopped and flung both hands high above his head. When he did this it hoisted his coat far enough for the men around Jim to see a six-gun with an elaborately carved handle.

He was still standing like that when horsemen became visible behind him. They also saw the man with upraised arms and the other men. Their leader, bundled inside a sheep-pelt coat hauled down to a walk, then stopped altogether. For ten seconds both sides considered the other before the man in the sheep-pelt coat said, 'Who the hell are you an' what was all the gunfire about?'

Ben Hobart did an unexpected thing; he walked toward the mounted man saying, 'Hello, Gordon. Glad to see you.'

The man in the sheep-pelt coat leaned with both hands atop the saddlehorn, was briefly silent then said, 'Ben! What the hell is goin' on?'

Hobart's reply was direct. 'I figured them cattle with a mule-shoe brand was yours. They busted out of the corral. Most likely they're scattered to hell an' back by now.'

The other man ignored Hobart's statement to repeat his question. 'What happened an' what're you doin' here?'

Ben turned. 'That there is Jim Welsh, them others is his riders, except one man who's the town marshal of Cedarville and that whiskery gent. His name's Marcus. He come with us from Fort Drum.' Hobart jerked a thumb in the direction of the man still holding both hands overhead. 'I got no idea who he is, but I can tell you the gang that rustled your mule-shoe cattle was goin' to sell them to a cow buyer, an' maybe that's him.'

The leader of the newcomers swung to the ground, peeled off a pair of roping gloves, looked back and nodded. His riders also dismounted. He approached the man with the carved-stocked six-gun and said, 'Put your hands down. Now then, who are you?'

The rumpled, stout man replied without hesitation. 'I'm Cal Billings from up north.'

The older man in the sheep-pelt coat said, 'A cattle buyer?'

Cal Billings fidgeted. 'I buy cattle, yes.'

'Stolen cattle, Mister Billings?'

The stout man's eyes skipped among the faces in front of him. 'I always get a bill of sale, Mister—?'

The stockman stood silently considering Cal Billings for a long time before he turned and addressed a hawk-faced man among his riders. 'You got a rope handy, Slim?'

The rider turned to free up his coiled lariat as Cal Billings ran his words together when he said, 'I didn't know them cattle was stolen. Mister Moody had a bill of sale for 'em. You can ask him. I'm tellin' you the gospel truth, Mister—'

'Mister Grundig, Gordon Grundig. Where is this Mister Moody?'

Four Feathers came limping around from the north side of the corral. Someone had used a belt to make a tourniquet half-way between the 'breed's hip and knee. He leaned against the corral when he said, 'Mister Moody's around yonder—dead.' The 'breed looked at Jim. 'This one's lyin'. He knew those cattle was stolen.'

Tad went over to help the 'breed who waved him off. 'I heard 'em talkin' before hell broke loose. He asked Moody when he could expect the next herd an' Moody said in about a month over in the Cedarville country. This lard bucket told Moody he was doin' real good. That he could peddle every head Moody could rustle.'

The grizzled cowman in the sheep-pelt coat faced Cal Billings in silence. After a moment he spoke again to that rider he had called Slim. 'Take this miserable son of a bitch an' hang him.'

Slim jerked his head and three of Grundig's six riders went toward the cattle buyer, who, desperate though he was, did a foolish thing. He grabbed for the fancy handled six-gun. The cowboy nearest behind him lunged, knocked

Billings sideways. He lost his balance and before he recovered it three Grundig riders had him with both arms twisted up his back. His face contorted in pain as he said, 'That In'jan's a damned liar. I got a bill of sale to prove it.' Tad Butler and Win Evans started for him. The Grundig riders swung Billings sideways as their boss stepped between the Long Bow men and the man his riders were holding. Jim Welsh spoke quietly. 'Mister Grundig, Four Feathers don't lie. He's been riding for me for some years. *He don't lie!*'

Grundig considered Jim briefly before nodding and gesturing for his riders to take Billings away. The cattle buyer raised his voice in pleas interspersed with curses and promises to tell all he knew about Moody and rustled cattle.

Grundig kept his back to the struggling man and addressed Jim Welsh. 'I've heard of your outfit. One of the biggest in the territory.' He shoved out a hand which Jim gripped and released.

While Billings was being tied to the horse he no longer offered to expose the rustling ring, instead he begged for his life.

The three riders led by the man called Slim led the horse with Billings atop it in the direction of the northerly woodlands. The others could hear him alternately swearing and begging for his life.

Four Feathers slid down the corral to the

ground. Tad and Ben Hobart went over. Hobart loosened the tourniquet a little, and after a moment tightened it again as he spoke aside to Tad.

'He can't ride. Go see if you can get a wagon down at the settlement.'

The chill had been increasing for some time. Men ducked down into coats and listened to livestock in the distance. Dawn was close; it had been a hectic night and they were tired all the way through.

Win Evans walked out a ways. His long-eared friend followed like a dog.

As yet no one had missed Barney. He came shuffling out of the easterly darkness herding a pair of unwashed, unkempt men in front. When he came up he eased down the dog and leathered his six-gun. 'They was hidin' in some rocks. Couldn't find their horses.' Barney went to lean on the corral, he was weary all the way through, dishevelled and sore from walking. 'I guess they can tell you all you want to know.' Barney saw Four Feathers slumped beside the corral, turned his back on the others and approached the 'breed, whose trousers were bloody. Barney knelt, produced a pony of whiskey and gave it to the 'breed. 'Found it in their camp by the fire. Take more'n a swallow. Where's Tad?'

'Gone to find a wagon.'

Win Evans walked back where Barney was kneeling, considered the 'breed and said, 'I

149

passed Tad headin' for the settlement.' The lawman knelt, wrinkled his nose and looked at Barney. 'You got some whiskey?'

Barney's answer was curt. 'Found a bottle out yonder. It's for Feathers. Go hunt up your own.'

Marshal Evans went over where Jim and the heavily coated, grizzled, Muleshoe G cowman were talking. Out of the corner of his eyes he saw riders approaching and turned. Grundig said, 'My men; they lynched that lyin', miserable, son of a bitching cattle buyer.'

Win went around to the north side of the corral, found Jep standing over a face-up dead man. Win stepped past, yanked an ivory-stocked gun from its holster and stood examining the weapon as he said, 'I always wanted a fancy one like this,' and walked away.

Pert came out of the night, stopped, looked from the rangeboss to the dead man and said, 'You shoot him?'

He shook his head. 'I got no idea who done it but I can't raise a tear.'

Pert knelt and rifled the corpse, came up with an elegant gold watch chain and a gold pocket watch. He also came up with a thick money-belt which had in part given Moody his paunchy appearance. As he stood up Pert opened one of the little pockets, held the belt up close and blew out a sigh of breath. 'Chock full of money,' he said, and offered the belt for Jep's inspection. The rangeboss handed the belt back. 'That'll maybe pay Hobart for the cattle they stole off him.'

'By my calculation there's enough here to pay Jim back too.' Pert looked down and said, 'Thank you—you no-good, cattle-stealin' bastard.'

The Long Bow men went in the direction of the little fires which were no longer burning. They found two rustlers who had been trampled to death and one with a little bloody circle in the middle of his forehead. They plundered them and got back to the corral about the time someone driving a rattling wagon from the direction of Freedom City could be heard.

When Tad came up he had a skinny, leathery man on the seat beside him. He did not introduce the man he simply jerked his thumb and told the others the man owned the wagon and team and would not let them go unless he went with them.

They went among the ruined camps, brought back blankets and ground-cloths, made a good bed and hoisted Four Feathers into it.

Mister Grundig went over to gaze in at the 'breed before going to the far side of the wagon where the owner was hunched inside a threadbare old blanket coat and handed the man some money. 'Take him down to Fort Drum, find someone who can patch him up an' don't leave there until he's looked after. You

151

understand?'

The scrawny villager pocketed the money, nodded and drove away. Barney roused himself, got his horse and followed the wagon. No one said anything about this. For a damned fact Barney was getting more and more like a mother hen.

Pert went after the horses they had left atop the timbered upthrust. When he returned they got mounted, herded their prisoners in front and started in the direction of Freedom City, where there were lights showing. The fight, which had not actually lasted very long, had roused everyone within miles.

Despite the obviousness of people being wide awake when the riders reached Freedom City only one man came out of a shanty. He let them halt without speaking a word. Behind him a tousled-headed youngster peeked past a cobbled-together wooden door. If Barney had been there he would have recognized the lad. The other Long Bow men probably did but no one heeded him. Mister Grundig spoke to the solitary villager. Around them the cold had increased and so had visibility. Not much, but enough so that it was possible to discern details which, in sunlight, would not look as forlorn and disreputable as they looked in false-dawn.

'There's about sixty head of cattle loose out yonder. They belong to me. My name's Grundig. They're branded Muleshoe G. For every one you can round up and corral I'll pay one dollar.' Grundig paused to stroke a stubbly chin with his gloved hand. 'You folks shy of meat, are you?'

The man still said nothing but nodded his head.

Mister Grundig said, 'Take two for butcherin'. That'll pay you folks for the bother of buryin' the dead an' tearin' down their corral. Is that fair enough?'

Still the villager did not speak and again he nodded his head.

As Grundig was shortening his reins he said, 'Don't destroy the corral until you got my cattle corralled. I'll send some riders for them directly.'

As the riders were beginning to move clear the youngster pushed out the door and stood with his father looking after them. The particular older rider was not among them and that worried him.

The prisoners were as tired as their captors; they walked ahead with dragging steps. No one offered to take them up behind a saddle. Mister Grundig, snug inside his sheep-pelt coat, told Jim Welsh they should hang the pair of rustlers as soon as they found some decent trees. Jim did not say anything but Ben Hobart did. 'Be a pleasure, Gordon.'

The cowman looked at Hobart. 'They raid you did they?'

'Made off with about forty head.'

Pert abruptly rode ahead and held forth the money-belt. For once he said something the riders approved of. 'Take out what you figure they cost you to replace.'

Everyone except Jep was astounded. Hobart hesitated until Pert also said, 'I got it off Moody.' He did not mention the big gold watch and chain. Jim passed the belt to Ben Hobart, who looped his reins and fumbled with the pockets. He drew forth two flattened pads of greenbacks. Jim watched Hobart count the money, thought he had taken about what replacement cattle would cost and accepted the belt when Hobart held it out to him. Jim made sure the little pockets were buttoned, and handed it back to Pert, who dropped back to ride with the others. One of the Grundig riders said, 'First time I ever seen a grave robber do a decent thing.'

Dawn was close but the cold remained unabated. When they had rooftops in sight one of the Grundig riders spoke to his boss. 'Them squatters ought to do real good between the critters you gave 'em an' the loose horses and camp-goods they find.'

Grundig's reply was made without the older man looking back. 'Folks like that have one streak of good luck for every twenty streaks they get of bad luck.' He watched Fort Drum fill out in detail before addressing Jim Welsh. 'We'll cut off from here, Mister Welsh, an' take them rustlers with us if you don't mind.'

Jim's reply was simple. 'You're welcome to 'em, Mister Grundig, an' we're obliged to you. If you hadn't showed up it might have ended different.'

Grundig glanced back at his riders, faced forward and said, 'We missed the cattle the day after they was rustled. Trackin' was easy, until it got too dark. After that, when we was at the settlement askin' around the fight broke out behind that knoll. Only thing those folks told us was there was a party of riders lay by west of the settlement until sundown. It didn't take much figurin'—they was either more rustlers or someone, like us, who was lookin' for cattle thieves.'

The Muleshoe G riders peeled off north of the Drum settlement heading south-west with a warming sun on their lee side. Jim led his party into the village where two women came forth to tell them their Indian was at the general store in the back room, and waited until the men had tied up to lead the way.

The storekeeper was as jumpy as a cat on a hot tin roof. Most of the Fort Drum residents were inside the store or outside on the plankwalk.

Barney met Jim in the store, silently led the way to a small, gloomy room that smelled of stocked food and dust. There were two hissing lamps, one on each side of the bed where Four Feathers watched his companions file in as long-faced as mules.

155

One of the attending women, matronly, pretty fifteen years back, arose and smoothed her apron as Jim told her who he and the others were. She held both hands clasped in front as she said, 'He's not fit to travel. At least not a-horseback, and that old wagon they brought him here in would keep the wound bleeding if he had to go much farther in it.'

They crowded around the bed. Four Feathers wanted to know what had happened after he was taken away. They told him and Pert held up the money-belt, grinning like a tame ape.

Four Feathers looked and acted normal but that fooled no one. He was as weak as a kitten. Jim left to seek a rig with springs under it. A large, awry-haired man said there was a decent rig in the area but, he said, there was a train due through heading south from Fort Laramie. He told Jim they would stop the train and when Jim looked sceptical the awry-haired man said, 'If we got to pile trees on the tracks, mister. We heard about what happened up yonder. We'll stop the train, take my word for it.'

12

A LONG WAY BACK

When Jim returned to the store and pushed his way through to the storeroom, the others were waiting. When he told them about the train Jep and Barney left to find a place to nap.

Tad found a bench, put it at bedside and smiled at the matronly woman. She smiled back but tentatively. Tad, of all of them, looked and smelled like something a pup would drag home from a tanyard.

Pert went out front where townsmen nailed him. He was a willing but an altogether reliable storyteller. Between answering questions he told the storekeeper which cans of tinned peaches and whatnot he wanted.

No one was sure when the southbound out of Laramie would arrive, but the general consensus was late afternoon. Pert took his purchases to the storeroom, handed them around and smiled at the horrified look on the matronly woman's face when they used clasp knives to punch holes, drank the syrup and ate the fruit.

Shortly before departing she looked at Four Feathers' wound, which was swollen, purplish in colour and had been disinfected with some white powder which stuck to the moist flesh. She reset the bandage, pulled up the covers and told the 'breed the bleeding had stopped. She also told him not to move the leg or the bleeding would start again.

After she left Jim sat on a pile of flour sacks. He was tired. He had been hungry too until he'd been handed one of Pert's tins.

The storekeeper came to the doorway, wrinkled his nose and announced that there was a wash-house out back. When all he got for this information was blank looks he also said the train would be along about three o'clock and it was running ahead of schedule.

Jim asked if the trainmen knew they were to stop at Fort Drum and got a reply he could probably have anticipated.

'They'll fill up with water from that tank north of town. We'll catch 'em up there an' tell 'em about you gents.'

Four Feathers slept; the woman returned and the Long Bow men went out front where a number of locals were still lingering. One of them, older, shrewd-eyed with a pouched cheek, spat aside then addressed Ben Hobart. 'Ain't you the feller rode with a Clarendon posse some time back?'

Ben considered the older man. 'You mean when there was a shoot-out?'

'Yes sir.'

'I was there,' Hobart said and turned his back on the older man, who tugged the sleeves

158

of two other men, led them up the roadway a fair distance then turned and talked steadily for almost five minutes. When he finished all three men turned and stared at Ben Hobart.

Shadows were forming when they heard a train northward. Jim led the group of men in the direction of the water tower. Pert, Tad and Jim were joined by puffy-eyed Barney and the rangeboss.

The train had two cattle cars behind a passenger car. The engine was noisily expelling steam as it slowed near the water tower.

A trainman shinnied aft of the engine and was reaching for the downspout when Pert loudly said, 'Hell, that's the same feller we come north with.'

The man reaching for the spout twisted to look down. He did not complete positioning the spout and yanking the release rope for several seconds, then he did those things and considered the small crowd below. Between the hissing engine and the gush of water he could not have been heard if he had spoken, which he didn't do, he just leaned up there wagging his head.

When he locked the downspout in an upraised position he climbed down and said, 'I knew when I got up this mornin' it was goin' to be a bad day. Where are your horses? We don't have no ramp an' one of the cars is full of cattle.'

'Do you stop at Kingsville?'

'Yes.'

'That's where our horses are . . . we'll pick 'em up there.'

That awry-haired man knew the trainman and called him by name. 'Ned; they got a wounded feller at the store that needs the doctor over in Clarendon.'

Another trainman appeared. This one wore a blue suit and a hat with a shiny visor. Across his middle was a gold chain which led to a pocket where his railroad watch was kept. He did not smile when he addressed the waterman. 'Ned, we're runnin' behind.'

Barney remembered this pompous individual and moved in front of him to say, 'Mister, we got a shot man needs a doctor.'

The blue-suited individual pulled out his watch, consulted it then said, 'Get him aboard. Where is he?'

'At the store.'

The pompous man scowled. 'Fetch him fast. We're runnin' behind.'

The awry-haired man called several villagers by name and led them back toward the settlement.

The blue-clad man scowled at the other trainman who said, 'Don't look at me. I didn't know they was here.'

Several other townsmen turned back to follow the men who had gone with the awry-haired man.

The party thinned until there were only Ben

Hobart, Thad Marcus and the Long Bow men. The man who had watered the engine fixed Marcus with a hostile glare. 'What'n hell's goin' on?' he asked and got a curt answer.

'These gents an' Gordon Grundig caught some rustlers up at the Freedom City shantytown. There was a hell of a fight. One of these fellers got shot.'

Win Evans had been staring at the pompous trainman. Now he spoke. 'Mister, you fellers been haulin' rustled cattle . . . you know a gent named Moody?'

'Burt Moody?'

'That's him,' the marshal replied. 'Well . . . he's dead back yonder . . . an' seems to me the railroad might have some explainin' to do.'

The pompous man said, 'Why? Our business is to haul passengers and freight—'

'An' stolen cattle?' Evans said gazing at the pompous man without blinking.

'Cattle is cattle,' the waterman growled and Win turned on him. 'Do you fellers ask to see bills of sale, or do you just load cattle anywhere they're corralled? You want to know what I think . . . I think your railroad's responsible for aidin' an' abettin' cattle thieves.'

The pompous railroader was on the point of replying angrily when that older man who had asked Hobart about a gun-fight, sidled up to the angry man in the blue suit, leaned and said, 'Mister, you got one foot on a banana

161

peel an' the other one in the grave. That man next to him is Ben Hobart.'

The pompous man was unimpressed but the waterman wasn't. He said, 'Leave it be,' to the pompous man and when it appeared his advice was not going to be heeded, he took him by the arm and walked him back down the engine where he released him and talked like a Dutch uncle. Once the pompous man looked back where Hobart was watching them both thumbs hooked in his shell-belt.

The railroad man walked down the cars, climbed aboard and did not reappear even when the villagers arrived carrying a loading chute.

Jim waited until he was satisfied the portable chute would be satisfactory, then sent Pert to help Win Evans fetch an animal.

Jep worried off a cud and cheeked it while watching the villagers grunt and strain to lock the loading chute into place, then he went over and spoke to Jim. 'Grundig'll hang them rustlers.'

Jim responded curtly, 'Saves us the trouble.'

Jep spat aside before also saying, 'There's still one to settle with,' and this time Jim faced his rangeboss.

'I know. We'd ought to make Clarendon by late in the day.'

The villagers stood on each side of the chute as Pert and Marshal Evans coaxed a long-faced mule up the ramp, then hoisted the chute clear and closed the door.

The waterman came back to ask Jim if he was ready. When he nodded the waterman pointed to a passenger car. 'Ride in there,' he said, and walked away.

It required almost another half-hour to get Four Feathers in the passenger car and settled on the floor under blankets because the seats could not be notched far enough back. All this was watched by two women, one old and hawk-faced, the other young and pretty. There were three male passengers. They neither moved nor made a sound as the unwashed, unshaven, weary-looking stockmen got aboard.

In fact none of the passengers even looked at the Long Bow men if they could avoid it, and when the train jerked and lunged, throttled off escaping steam and made grinding sounds as it moved, the passenger car might as well have been empty except for Jim Welsh and his companions, which suited them. Even Four Feathers slept. His friends sprawled anywhere they felt like doing it and also slept.

Once, the pompous trainman came to the door of the passenger car, stopped then turned back.

Barney could have been yanked over rocky ground by wild horses before he would have admitted it, but the gentle rocking motion of the train as much as the soporific effect of its wheels clicking over rails put him into probably the deepest and most restful time of his life.

By the time they reached Clarendon the sun was sinking, the pre-evening had shadows and most folks were at supper. They off-loaded the horses, ignored the man with the blue eyeshade who stepped out to watch, and led their animals to the livery barn to be fed, watered and cuffed. They then went directly to the café where the caféman looked shocked at their appearance, but had the good sense to feed them without speaking. There were other diners, and among them was the constable. They all ate supper in silence but when the constable was finished he shucked coin atop the counter, hitched at his britches and walked up behind Jim Welsh. 'Telegraph told us you was comin', Mister Welsh. Wasn't there a couple of rustlers with you?'

Ben Hobart turned slowly. He smiled. At first the constable did not recognize him. When he did he said, 'Ben! I met your missus a couple of days back. She told me about them rustled cattle an' said you went lookin' for 'em.'

As they shook hands Hobart said, 'I as good as got the cattle back.'

'Is that a fact? Whereabouts?'

'Over near a settlement called Freedom City.'

Barney called for another plate and when it came he left the café with it, something the constable saw. He looked back at Hobart. 'You got a sick 'un, have you?'

'A Long Bow rider. He got winged in the leg. We left him at the livery barn.' Hobart smiled again. 'Next time I'm in town I'll tell you all about it. You goin' to be in town tonight?'

The constable shook his head. 'I got to go out to the Duffy place. Duffy heard about you gettin' raided an' thinks he lost some cattle too.' The constable sighed. 'You know Alec Duffy?' When Hobart nodded the lawman rolled his eyes. 'If we go two weeks without rain he calls it a drought. When his wife calved he liked to drove the mid-wife crazy. It's a long ride an' it'll be cold before I get back, but if I don't go Duffy'll tell folks I don't do my job.'

Jim and the others had listened to this conversation and when the constable departed Ben Hobart looked down the counter and smiled.

They filled up, had refills for their coffee cups, went outside where shadows were thickening and Pert was looking at the red-brick bank building when he said, 'It ain't open this late is it?'

No one answered but Ben Hobart spoke to Jim in a low tone. 'He lives at the rooming-house.' As they started in that direction Pert spoke again, 'Suppose he ain't there?'

The rooming-house porch was sagging with wood-rot, the door was not locked and whined on dry springs when it was opened. If Barney had been with them he would have had something to say about that.

The parlour was to the right of the hallway. When they came abreast of its doorless wide opening an old man reading a newspaper and smoking a cigar looked up. His eyes widened. His arms appeared to be frozen, he did not lower the newspaper.

Jim asked for directions to the banker's room and the old man gave them swiftly. 'Down the hall, last door on the right.'

Jim asked another question. 'Do you know if he's in there?'

'Yes sir, he's in there. I saw him go past a few minutes ago. He was hurrying. I called good evening. He never even looked around.'

Jep leaned to whisper to Jim. 'I'll go around back,' he said, and returned to the rickety porch.

The hallway was dingy with a threadbare runner and hanging overhead lamp mid-way which no one had cleaned. Soot inside the mantle obscured most light except upwards.

Jim paused outside the last room on the right side to listen. Whoever was in there was noisily busy whatever he was doing.

Jim closed a fist around the doorknob and gently twisted. The door was locked. He just as gently released the knob, motioned for leeway and hit the door so hard it was torn off its lower hinge.

Arthur Knowlton froze. He had a pair of

saddle-bags and a satchel on the bed. He had been filling the saddle-bags when the door burst open. As Jim pushed inside and would have spoken the Clarendon banker half twisted away, and twisted back with an under-and-over derringer in his right fist. He had a thumb on the knurled hammer to draw it back before firing when Ben Hobart shot him through the body. The noise was thunderous and a man in slippers and an old robe who had been awakened when the door was broken open, stopped stone-still in the hallway. Tad looked out and saw him. Tad palmed his six-gun. For five seconds they looked at each other then the man in the robe went swiftly into a nearby room and closed the door.

They flung the satchel and saddle-bags on the floor, put the banker on the bed and with Jim looking down Knowlton said, 'Get the doctor.' He had both hands over a bloody wound in his soft parts.

Pert opened the satchel and whistled. Jim did not look but Hobart did, and softly said, 'Jim.'

Welsh turned, saw the money, turned back and spoke to the wounded man. 'Cleaned out the bank, Art?'

'That's my money.'

'Moody give it to you? Moody's dead.'

The wounded man did not appear to be in much pain but he was bleeding like a gut-shot bear. He rolled his eyes around the room then closed them. He was still breathing, and bleeding.

Hobart picked up the bellygun, snapped it open, removed the bullets, leaned and dropped them on Knowlton, whose eyes opened, but only part way.

Jim leaned down. 'Moody's dead, some of his riders got killed, some got hanged, including a buyer named Billings. Did you know him?'

There was no answer. A dowdy, large, hatchet-faced woman wrapped in an old robe pushed past Tad and stopped at the sight of the blood which had spread to the blankets.

She leaned, held Knowlton's wrist briefly, then gently placed the arm on his chest as she straightened up to put a sulphurous look on Jim Welsh. 'Who the hell are you an' what right you got to bust into a man's room an' shoot him?'

Ben Hobart spoke to the woman. 'Nettie, he robbed the bank an' was workin' with cattle rustlers.'

The woman glared at Hobart. 'Ben,' she exclaimed, 'I don't believe a word you said.'

Hobart turned the woman by the arm so she could see the opened satchel. She looked a long time before facing Hobart. 'From the bank?'

Ben nodded and the woman turned fiercely toward the man on the bed. 'My savings too, Art? I'd have shot you myself.'

Jim shook his head at the woman as he said, 'He can't hear you.'

On their way out of the rooming-house Jim glanced in as he passed the parlour. The old man was still sitting there, still holding his newspaper as though both elbows were inflexibly bent, his eyes fixed on the stained, unkempt strangers, unable to utter a word if the salvation of his soul had depended on it.

Pert was the last man to pass, he looked in and grinned at the old man. Pert had a satchel in one hand and a pair of saddle-bags in the other.

People had heard the gunshot; they had also seen those hard-looking strangers go to the rooming-house before the shooting and watched from behind curtained windows as the strangers walked in the direction of the livery barn.

Down there the nighthawk, a gangling, ragged youth, had also heard the gunshot and when the Long Bow men came into the feebly lighted run he had to go to a wall bench and sit down.

He knew more than other folks in Clarendon. He had given the wounded 'breed a bottle of popskull from the liveryman's desk drawer and in exchange for this kindness Four Feathers had told him the entire story from start to finish.

Ben Hobart tapped Jim on the shoulder, shoved out his hand and said, 'I'm obliged,

Mister Welsh. If you're ever down this way again an' need anythin'—anythin' at all—folks can tell you where my ranch is.'

As Hobart walked past Jep he slapped the rangeboss lightly on the shoulder. Barney, in the harness-room door, called after Hobart, 'You're a good man to ride the rims with.'

Hobart turned and smiled. 'For a feller your age you done better'n most would have done. Come look me up sometime.'

Barney nodded. 'I'll do that. Mister Hobart, you know how fellers live to my age? They keep their powder horn higher'n their shot pouch.'

Hobart laughed, the only time any of them had heard him do that.

Jim talked to the nighthawk who led them out back to the wagon shed where Jim told the lad to bring in the team and harness it. He told the others to filch hay for bedding. All of them lifted Four Feathers, kept the blanket taut, got him gently and carefully settled in the hay, and Four Feathers clung to the liveryman's bottle as though his life depended on it. He bled, but only around the edges of his enormously swollen upper leg.

They hitched the team. Jim told the speechless nighthawk who he was and that he'd return the outfit within a few days, and to tell the constable he would have something for him when he returned, then climbed to the seat, talked up the horses and drove northward out of Clarendon with dumbfounded people watching from a dozen hidden places.

They had a long ride. Tad and Barney led Four Feathers' and Jim's horses. Every now and then Barney would edge close to the wagon and look down in. The last time he did this Four Feathers held up the bottle and burst into the lyrics of *The Battle Hymn of the Republic*.

At the tail-end of the cavalcade, Marshal Evans rode, occasionally looking back where a solemn-faced mule was following him.